OUR SONG

flirt

Read the entire Flirt series!

FLIRT

OUR SONG

A. DESTINY AND ELIZABETH LENHARD

SIMON PULSE

NEW YORK   LONDON   TORONTO   SYDNEY   NEW DELHI

SIMON PULSE

An imprint of Simon & Schuster Children's Publishing Division

1230 Avenue of the Americas, New York, New York 10020

This Simon Pulse paperback edition July 2015

Text copyright © 2015 by Simon & Schuster, Inc.

Cover photograph copyright © 2015 by Justin Pumfrey/Getty Images

All rights reserved, including the right of reproduction in whole or in part in any form.

SIMON PULSE and colophon are registered trademarks of Simon & Schuster, Inc.

For information about special discounts for bulk purchases, please contact Simon & Schuster Special Sales at 1-866-506-1949 or business@simonandschuster.com.

The Simon & Schuster Speakers Bureau can bring authors to your live event. For more information or to book an event contact the Simon & Schuster Speakers Bureau at 1-866-248-3049 or visit our website at www.simonspeakers.com.

Designed by Regina Flath

The text of this book was set in Adobe Caslon Pro.

Manufactured in the United States of America

10 9 8 7 6 5 4 3 2 1

Library of Congress Cataloging-in-Publication Data

Destiny, A.

Our song / by A. Destiny and Elizabeth Lenhard.

pages cm.—(Flirt)

Summary: "When fifteen-year-old Nell is forced to go to folk camp for the summer, she eventually falls back in love with her musical roots, and possibly with fellow musician, Jacob"—Provided by publisher.

ISBN 978-1-4424-8406-1 (pbk. : alk. paper) ISBN 978-1-4424-8408-5 (ebook) [1. Camps—Fiction. 2. Love—Fiction. 3. Music—Fiction.] I. Lenhard, Elizabeth. II. Title.

PZ7.D475Ou 2015

[Fic]—dc23

2014030457

Chapter ● One

At the Winnie C. Camden Folk School, all the sounds are peaceful and antique—the *pling, pling, pling* of hammer dulcimers, the sleepy grind of katydids, the *whoosh* of fire in forges and kilns. While people are here, whether it's for a weekend workshop or an entire month of quilting or wildflower painting, they will themselves to become antique too. They pretend they've never heard of Twitter or texting. Somebody *always* seems to be singing, *"'Tis the gift to be simple, 'tis the gift to be free . . ."* But me? When I arrived at Camden on the second day of June, my summer barely begun, I made way too much noise. I didn't mean to. (Not entirely, anyway.) But I was driving my grandma's stiff and wheezy van, lumbering from too much cargo. The slightest turn of the steering wheel in the Camden parking lot unleashed a spray of gravel. And when I'd parked and stumbled out of the driver's seat—stiff and sore after the four-hour journey from Atlanta to North Carolina—I accidentally slammed my door.

At least, I *think* it was an accident.

Maybe I was just bad with cars. I'd only had my learner's permit for three weeks.

"Please remind me *why* I agreed to let you drive?" my grandma asked as she creaked out of the passenger seat and shuffled toward the back of the van.

I circled around too, meeting Nanny by the rear door.

"Because you have an iron stomach, and *I* always get carsick up here?" I offered. Camden lay in a valley blockaded on all sides by mountains. The only way to reach it was along nauseatingly twisty roads.

"Or maybe," I suggested, smiling slyly as I leaned against our van's dented bumper, "you feel terrible for dragging me to no-Wi-Fi purgatory for the entire summer."

"Well, let me think on that," Nanny said, tapping a shortnailed fingertip against her pursed lips. "Do I feel bad for bringing you here for four weeks out of your *nine-week* summer? Do I feel guilty for asking you to assist in my fiddle class after being *your* one and only music teacher since you were three?"

I squirmed as Nanny moved her finger to her chin and pretended to give these questions serious consideration.

"Do I feel sorry for you," she went on, "because you broke curfew one too many times and your parents sent you here, to one of the most beautiful places on earth, as 'punishment'?"

Nanny made exaggerated air quotes with her fingers.

I folded my arms and sighed. I should have known not to give my grandma that easy opening. Maybe it was being a musician that gave her such perfect pitch for sarcasm. Once she got on a roll, she could improv forever.

Nanny gazed at the sky and mock-contemplated for another beat before she looked at me and grinned.

"Nope, my conscience is clear," she said. "But thank you for your concern, Nellie."

I rolled my eyes but couldn't stifle a tiny snort as I popped open the rear door. That was another talent of Nanny's. She could make me laugh even as she was doing something hideously parental like carting me off to folk music jail and calling me "Nellie" instead of Nell.

I started to pull our fiddle cases and bags out of the van, but before I could hand anything to Nanny, she'd set off across the parking lot, stretching her wiry arms over her head.

"What about our stuff?" I called after her.

Still walking, she tossed her answer over her shoulder.

"We'll get it after we check in."

There was an eagerness, even a little breathlessness, in her scratchy voice.

I'd almost forgotten that, as full of dread as I was about this summer, that's how excited Nanny was. She'd been teaching here—converting beginning violin students into improvising, hoe-downing, out-and-out fiddlers—for longer than I'd been alive. Only birth or death kept her from her Camden summers—literally. She'd stayed home the summer that I was born fifteen years ago, and then again when my brother Carl arrived.

Then, when Carl was four and I was nine, my grandfather got sick, very sick. Nanny canceled her month at Camden once again. A few weeks later, PawPaw died. That's when Camden came to Nanny. In the over-air-conditioned funeral home, one of the textile teachers draped Nanny's shoulders in a beautiful hand-knitted shawl. A couple of wood-carvers spent a whole night etching gorgeous designs into PawPaw's simple casket. And oh, the music. The music never stopped.

That helped most of all. Because in our family, music is the constant, the normal. Somebody is always picking or bowing, strumming or singing. On any given day in our house—and in Nanny's down the street—there are recordings happening in the basement and lessons being conducted in the front parlor. Dinner parties don't end with dessert but with front-porch jam sessions. Nanny, my parents, and their many musician friends stick to Irish, Appalachian, folk, and roots music, anything so long as it's really old. Bonus points if the lyrics involve coal miners with black lung or mothers dying in childbirth.

The strumming, singing, plinking is so constant, I barely hear it anymore. Music is the old framed photos that cover our bungalow walls, our faded rag rugs, and our tarnished, mismatched silverware—treasures to some, wallpaper to me.

Maybe that's why, as I followed Nanny onto the student-crowded lawn in front of the Camden lodge, it took me a moment to realize that somebody was playing a fiddle. It only registered when I saw Nanny veer away from the beeline she'd been making to the lodge. Then I noticed other students milling around the lawn cocking their heads, grinning, and following Nanny to a circle that had gathered around the musician playing the song. The tune was clear, sweet, strong, and of course, very vintage.

From the outskirts of the small crowd that had gathered, I couldn't see the fiddler. I could only glimpse the tip of his or her violin bow bobbing gracefully against the sky. But I didn't mind. I took a step back so I could eye the spectators instead.

Camden was one of those "ages nine to ninety-nine!" kind of places, so I wasn't surprised to see some earth mamas with long braids trailing down their backs, men in beards and plaid, and grandparent types wearing sensible sandals and sun hats. A lot of the kids were just that—kids. They looked a lot more like my ten-year-old brother than like me. They were probably here because they dreamed of being Laura Ingalls Wilder or Johnny Tremain. I knew this because when I was a little kid and came to Camden every other summer or so, *I'd* wanted to be Anne of Green Gables.

But soon after that, I'd started to find the Camden school too earnest, too stifling. It was the only place, outside of Santa's workshop, that I associated with the word "jolly."

There were clearly plenty of teenagers here who didn't feel

the same way. A few of them were in this group listening to the fiddler. There were two guys with patchy facial hair, wearing serious hiking boots and backpacks elaborately networked with canteens and compasses.

There was also a girl who looked about my age. Her pink cheeks looked freshly scrubbed. Her long, sand-colored hair was plaited into braids that snaked out from beneath a red bandanna. She wore black cargo shorts and white clogs.

Since she was engrossed in the violin music, I could stare at her and wonder which class she was taking. She didn't seem like a spinning/knitting type—they always wore flowing layers and smelled faintly of sheep. Maybe she was a quilter or a basket weaver? Or—

Soap, I decided with a nod. That had to be it. She was here to make beautiful, scented soaps molded into the shapes of flowers and fawns and woodland mushrooms.

Having made up my mind about Soap Girl, I turned in the other direction. My eyes connected immediately with those of another teenage girl. She'd taken a step back from the circle and was clearly sizing *me* up.

I gave her a cringing smile.

Caught me, I mouthed.

She laughed and headed toward me.

Or should I say, she *wafted* toward me. Everything about this girl was light and fluttery, from her long black hair—a cascade of glossy, tight ringlets—to her flowing, ankle-skimming skirt. Her skin wasn't just brown—it was brown with golden undertones. The girl practically glowed.

When she reached me, she gave me a mischievous smile.

"You were totally judging that girl over there, weren't you?" she said.

"Um," I said sheepishly. "I think *judging* is kind of a harsh way to put it, but . . ."

"What class do you think she's taking?" the girl asked.

"Soap making," I said quickly. "Definitely soap making."

"See?" she said, a gleeful bubble in her voice. "You're wrong. I asked her a few minutes ago, and she's taking canning."

"Canning?"

"Oh, it's a new class Camden added," the girl said with a graceful flick of her hand. "You know, jams, jellies, pickles. Anything you can put in a jar. I'm from New York, and it's *the* thing up there. You can't throw a rock without hitting somebody in a slouchy hat carrying a box of mason jars. And probably a messenger bag full of bacon. Not that I would *ever* . . ."

"Throw a rock at somebody?" I asked. I was kind of having a hard time following this girl. For somebody who looked so Zen and wispy, she sure talked fast.

"*Or* eat bacon," she replied. "Anyway, I'm Annabelle. I'm taking pottery."

Of course *you're taking pottery,* I thought, suppressing a giggle. But what I said out loud was, "Oh, cool. Pottery's fun."

"Oh, it's more than fun," she said. Then she launched into an explanation of her choice, talking so excitedly that I could make out only a few snatched phrases.

"I need to *live* before I head to college in the fall . . . reach deep into my inner being . . . suck the marrow out of life . . . not just a *taker*, you know, but a *maker*. . . . I'm taking pottery as a way to get back to the earth. . . ."

When she seemed to be done with her monologue—which had more twists and turns to it than a mountain road—I smiled, nodded hard, and said, "That's great! You go!"

Luckily, Annabelle didn't see my vague response for what it was: *I have no idea what you just said.*

Instead she clasped her hands in front of her chest and looked a bit misty-eyed as she said, "Thank you for that validation. *Really.*"

"Um, no problem," I said. "By the way, I'm Nell."

"No. Way," Annabelle said, her dark eyes widening. I noticed that her lashes were as lush and curly as her hair.

"Yes, Nell," I sighed. "I know it must sound like a hopelessly hillbilly name, especially to someone from New York. My family—"

"Nell," Annabelle said with a frown. "First of all, *never* apologize for your name. Your name is an *essential* part of your identity. Second of all, if you're Nell Finlayson, you're my roommate!"

I blinked.

"Well, I am Nell Finlayson," I said, "so I guess I am. Your roommate, I mean."

As I said this, I felt a mixture of excitement and panic.

Annabelle clearly had what adults called a "strong personality." The thing is, I'm pretty sure the adults hardly ever mean that as a compliment.

"So, Nell, how old are you?" Annabelle demanded bluntly.

"Fifteen," I said.

"I'm two years older than you," she replied. "Which means, I'm in a position to give you some advice."

"More advice, you mean?" I said, before I could stop myself.

Annabelle didn't seem to notice. Instead she looped her arm through mine. We were about the same height, five foot seven, but next to her willowy goldenness, I felt washed-out and shriveled. Her clothes were a rippling rainbow of plum and teal, mustard and aqua. Meanwhile, my skinny capris were dark gray, and my tank top was the brooding color of an avocado peel. My hair— freshly blunt cut and flatironed to a crisp—was dyed black. Only my feet had a bit of brightness to them. I was wearing my favorite acid-yellow, pointy-toed flats.

"Check out *that*," Annabelle ordered me. She pointed at the disembodied fiddle bow, which was still doing its little dance in the center of the crowd.

I glanced at it, then shrugged at Annabelle.

"I'm not talking about the instrument," Annabelle insisted. She grabbed me by the shoulders and shuffled me sideways until we were able to peek through a break in the crowd. "I'm talking about the *player!*"

I followed her gaze to the musician.

And then I caught my breath.

The fiddler was a boy.

A boy who was clearly in high school. (His cutoff khakis, orange-and-green sneakers, and T-shirt that said ASHWOOD HIGH SCHOOL CROSS-COUNTRY were hints.)

I might have also noticed that the boy's eyes were a deep, beautiful blue. You could see the color even though he was wearing glasses with chunky black frames. His glossy, dark-brown hair flopped over his forehead in a particularly cute way. His nose had just a hint of a bump in the bridge, and I could tell that his torso was long and slim beneath his faded yellow T-shirt.

And, oh yeah, his playing was beautiful too. Maybe even a notch above boring. His style was studied, sure. His rhythms were too even and his transitions were too careful to be untrained. He was clearly one of those Practicers that Nanny had always wanted me to be (but that I never had been).

But he also had talent.

No, more than that—he had the Joy.

The Joy makes you play until your fingertips are worn with deep, painful grooves.

The Joy makes you listen to all 102 versions of "Hallelujah" until you can decide which interpretation you love the best, even if it drives the rest of your family crazy.

And the Joy makes your face contort into funny expressions as you play.

I couldn't help but notice that even while this boy was

grimacing and waggling his eyebrows during the climax of his song, he still looked pretty good.

And when he stopped playing? When his thick eyebrows settled into place, his forehead unscrunched, and his pursed lips widened into a smile while the crowd applauded for him?

Well, then he became ridiculously good-looking.

"See what I'm talking about?" Annabelle said.

I opened my mouth and closed it again. How could I tell Annabelle that even if he was really, *really* good-looking, I could never be interested in someone who'd so clearly drunk the Camden Kool-Aid?

If I said that, I'd basically be insulting everybody who was there, including her.

So I just shrugged and said, "Um, yeah, nice fiddling."

"Nice?! That was *lovely.*" Nanny had appeared at our side. "That young man had *better* be in our class."

"*Our* class?" Annabelle inquired, blinking inquisitively at my grandmother.

"Nanny, this is Annabelle," I said. "We just figured out that we're roommates."

I turned back to Annabelle. "My grandma is one of Camden's fiddle teachers."

"And Nell is going to be my assistant," Nanny said proudly.

"Uh, yeah," I confirmed, trying not to sound morose.

Annabelle looked from me to Nanny, then back to me.

"*Interesting,*" she said.

Then she glanced at the dispersing circle of music lovers.

"And, hmm, I think it's about to get even more so."

"Huh?" I said.

I followed her gaze to the fiddler. This time, *he* was the one staring—with wide eyes and a sudden mottled blush on his neck—at me!

Chapter ● Two

After a moment of hesitation, the boy began coming my way.

I had no idea how I felt about this.

But the fact is, when a very good-looking boy walks toward you, looking all blotchy and thunderstruck, you can't help but give your hair a frantic pat and try to arrange your face into an aloof-yet-adorable expression. It's like a Darwinian imperative.

In this case, it also turned out to be completely unnecessary. Because after the boy reached me . . . he kept right on going! He only came to a nervous halt when he reached Nanny.

"Are you Annie Finlayson?" the boy asked. His voice—a tenor with a hint of a rasp to it—trembled a bit.

Nanny grinned and stuck out her hand.

"That I am," she said. "And *you* better be taking my fiddle class."

"That's the whole reason I'm here!" the boy blurted, still staring at Nanny (and still completely oblivious to me). "I mean, that's why I signed up for the June session instead of the July one. To study with you."

I tried hard not to roll my eyes. Then I glanced at Annabelle. She looked like she was trying hard not to laugh. This sealed the deal—I officially liked my new roommate. I leaned over to whisper in her ear.

"Want to help me haul my stuff to our room?" I pointed toward the parking lot.

But before we could sneak away, Nanny squeezed my arm and beamed at me.

"You know, my granddaughter Nell is a fiddler too," she told the boy.

Finally, *finally*, he seemed to notice that the great Annie Finlayson had a sidekick.

"Nell Finlayson," he stated. He looked at me for a beat too long. He smiled, a close-lipped, small, and unreadable smile. "You're not what I would have expected."

"How could you expect anything," I wondered, "when you didn't know I existed until five seconds ago?"

Because it's not like you noticed me or anything, I thought.

"Well, I mean, I kind of did know of you," the boy said. The blotches on his neck were starting to bloom again. "Your name is on most of the *Finlaysons* albums."

I'd played backup fiddle on a lot of my family's recordings, mostly when a session musician failed to show, or they just needed another layer of sound in the background. So it was true, my name was on a lot of their albums, deeply embedded in the liner notes in tiny, tiny print.

It was kind of weird that this guy knew that.

"Okay," the boy said, taking a deep, shuddering breath, "that sounded kind of creepy."

"Gotta agree with you there," I said, but I couldn't help but smile at him. How was it possible that his anxiety-flushed neck was so cute?

"I'm just—" He stared down at the fiddle in his arms, as if he was begging it for a bailout. "I like your family's music. And I swear I'm not a stalker in any way."

"Other than stalking my grandmother all the way to the Camden School," I teased, "from . . ."

"Connecticut," the boy said miserably. "Which, yes, is very far away. Okay, I guess I am a creepy, long-distance stalker."

"Aw, sweetheart," Nanny assured him, "you're a *fan*. I'm flattered. Don't let Nell make you feel self-conscious. She thinks fiddling is about as everyday as making toast."

"But it isn't!" the boy insisted to me. "Without your grandma and your parents, there're all these Appalachian songs that would have just disappeared! But they recorded them and even made sheet music for them so they're preserved for history."

I didn't respond. What are you supposed to say when

somebody tells you something that, of course, you already knew?

Before my silence got too awkward, Nanny jumped in.

"Well, bless your heart," she said to the boy. "That sounds like a speech you've made before."

"To my dad," he admitted. "He wanted me to stay up north this summer. You know, be a lifeguard and play baseball like my older brother. He's, um, not exactly a music guy."

"Maybe you should try different music," I murmured.

I heard another stifled snort come from Annabelle, who was standing just behind me.

"What was that, Nell, darlin'?" Nanny asked, smiling at me.

"Oh, nothing," I said while Annabelle grinned.

"So what's the difference between a violin and a fiddle anyway?" she asked. "I've always wondered."

"Oh, there's no difference, really," Nanny said. "A violin is a fiddle and a fiddle is a violin, especially when you're feeling fancy."

"But all violin-playing is *not* fiddling," the boy pointed out. Fiddle music is so *alive*. And it's so connected to a place. To *this* place. I still can't believe I'm here."

Then he turned to me.

"So," he asked me, "are you taking your grandma's class too?"

"Not exactly."

I glanced at Nanny. *You can explain this one,* I telegraphed to her.

Throughout this whole exchange, Nanny had been beaming, giddy to be at Camden with her granddaughter, even if her granddaughter was a bit on the sulky side.

But when I challenged her like that, her smile suddenly faded, and it was as dramatic as a dark cloud obscuring the sun.

My heart gave a guilty lurch.

Here's the thing about Nanny. She rarely misses an opportunity to tease me. She never lets me get away with being a brat or a drama queen (or as my parents like to call it, being fifteen).

But she also adores me. More than anything. Maybe even more than music. She would do just about anything for me.

And she could clearly see in my face what I wanted from her.

Or rather, what I *didn't* want.

I didn't want to be Anne of Green Gables anymore. I didn't really want to be Nell Finlayson of the liner notes either. And I *definitely* didn't want to spend my summer (okay, *half* my summer) helping fiddle students scratch out "Britches Full of Stitches" and "The Irish Washerwoman."

I'd been saying as much for weeks. But for some reason, *this* was the moment that Nanny finally heard me; this moment when I hadn't said a word.

Shooting me a wistful look, Nanny told the boy, "Nell *was* going to assist me in my class. But . . ."

I held my breath.

"But I think there's been a change of plans," Nanny finished.

I don't know why she did it.

Maybe she was taking pity on me because I was invisible to the opposite sex and looked like a raisin next to my glamorous new roommate.

Maybe she didn't want to hear me sulk all summer.

Or maybe she was finally starting to understand this fact about me: I may have played the fiddle since I was three. I may have played passable backup on the *Finlaysons* albums. I may even have had musical talent, or whatever.

But I didn't have the Joy.

I squeezed Nanny's hand, thanking her for finally getting this. Then I turned to the boy to explain.

"It's just that . . . music isn't really my thing."

"Even though you're basically a professional?" he said with an incredulous laugh. "Even though you're a Finlayson?"

"Well, I don't have a choice about *that* stuff," I replied. "Do I, Nanny?"

"I guess not," she replied. "It's our family business. I don't think it would have occurred to us *not* to involve you kids in it. To us, that was as important as teaching you to read."

The boy's face went slack and his eyes went dreamy—half-incredulous, half-longing. You'd have thought Nanny told him I'd been raised on a diet of candy and rainbows or I was the reincarnation of June Carter Cash.

Rather than disappoint this guy with the truth, I decided to squirm my way out of the conversation entirely.

"Speaking of reading," I said, way too brightly, "I just remembered I left my e-reader in the van. I need to go get it before it fries in this heat. My camera's in there too. Annabelle was just going to help me, right?"

"Well," she said, "actually, I've kind of run out of time. I want to do a smudging ceremony in our room before lunch."

"A *what*?" I asked her.

"See, it's all about good energy . . . ," Annabelle began. She launched into a convoluted history of "cleansing" a room with a tuft of burning sage. Again, I only understood snatches of what she was saying:

". . . sacred Native American ritual . . . the perfect meeting of earth, wind, and fire . . . and let's not forget about the importance of feng shui . . ."

As much as I liked Annabelle, I could tell we were going to have a lot of late-night conversations about the meaning of life and other "deep" things I knew nothing about.

I was also pretty sure our room was going to stink after she'd filled it with sage smoke.

When Annabelle finally paused to take a breath, Nanny nodded politely and said, "That's . . . fascinating, dear."

And the boy?

Snort.

Now *he* was trying not to laugh. He passed his hand over his mouth as if to wipe his giggle away. But his full lips still twitched and his eyes looked squinty and sparkly behind his glasses. They were also directed, not at Annabelle, but at me! I had a feeling he knew exactly how squirmy I felt listening to Annabelle's unintelligible feng shui talk.

"What's your name, anyway?" I asked him. It sounded more

blunt than I'd intended, but it did a good job of distracting him from silently mocking me.

"Oh, right," he said, shaking his head. "I'm Jacob. Jacob MacEvoy."

"Well, it's *so* nice to meet you," Nanny said, reaching up and patting his shoulder. He was only a few inches taller than me, but he positively towered over my tiny grandmother.

Then Nanny gave me a quick kiss on the cheek before hustling off to the lodge. The kiss felt an awful lot like a good-bye, even though we'd just arrived here.

"Sure you don't want to join me for the smudging?" Annabelle asked me as she, too, turned to leave.

"Um, I'd better get my stuff out of the van," I said, trying to look as if I'd pondered the opportunity for more than half a second.

And then it was just me and the boy—Jacob.

"Okay, well," I said awkwardly, "see you around."

"If not in fiddle class," he replied. Was that a smile tugging at one corner of his mouth?

"Uh, right. Not there."

I felt like there was more I should say—but I had no idea what. So I just gave him a limp wave that made me feel more raisinish than ever. Then I headed back to the parking lot.

That was the moment when I should have felt elated, like a bird out of its cage. I'd been freed from *endless* hours in Nanny's classroom.

Although, when I thought about it, Nanny's classroom was actually pretty cozy. It was a little cabin on the fringe of Camden's campus. The vaulted ceiling was paneled with knotty pine planks, and there were faded, flowery curtains in every window. They fluttered in the breeze of the many ceiling fans, which made it seem like they were dancing to the students' music.

Ah, the students, I thought. *That's the best part of this deal. All those terrible renditions of "Scarborough Fair" and "An Irish Jig" that I won't have to listen to over and over and over.*

Even if one of the students had already proven himself to be pretty good.

And even if he did have that intriguingly imperfect nose. And lips that were just a little too red and pretty for a boy's. And ropy muscles in his forearms that rippled when he played his violin.

I reached the van and popped the rear door open. Of course, the first thing I saw was my fiddle case. It was a battered wooden case, painted black-cherry red. It had been my grandfather's before it was mine. It was covered in old travel decals from Mississippi Delta, Sarasota, and Mobile. Seeing it there, waiting for me, gave me a hollow feeling in my stomach I couldn't quite identify.

Was I feeling guilty for bailing on Nanny's fiddle class?

Or was that empty belly a sign of . . . regret? Once again the image of Jacob's face flashed in my head.

"Oh, please!" I muttered to myself. I shoved the fiddle out of the way and instead grabbed my camera case, my backpack, and my bulging suitcase. "I'm just hungry."

I slammed the van door and hurried back toward the lodge. At least, I tried to hurry.

My overstuffed suitcase's wheels sank into the gravel of the parking lot and refused to turn. I ended up having to shuffle/drag it until I reached the grass, which made it only slightly more rollable.

Free as a bird? I thought as I dragged my heavy load up the hill. *Maybe not quite.*

Chapter ● Three

Inside the lodge, the sign-in table was set up in the lounge, a dim, cozy space that hadn't changed even the tiniest bit since I'd started coming to Camden as a kid. The elaborate quilts, God's eyes, and yellowed photos on the wood-paneled walls—they were all there. The chairs and love seats were still saggy and faded, with afghans tossed over their worn spots. Massive ceiling fans whirred lazily.

The lounge milled with students lugging suitcases of their own and clutching sheaves of registration forms.

I stepped up to the rustic-looking table at the front of the line. The table was, of course, handmade by Camden students out of wood from local poplar trees (according to a little gold plaque embedded in the table's edge). Behind it sat a white-haired lady who lit up at the sight of me.

"Nell Finlayson!" she chirped. Her voice, throaty and warbling, made me think of a puff-chested mama bird. "I'm Dorothy Teagle, the director of Camden. I've known your grandma for years and years and *years*. Oh, we're *so* excited to have you back. You know, I remember the last time you were here. You had that silky blond hair hanging down your back. *So* pretty."

"Thanks," I muttered. Reflexively I smoothed down my current hairdo, which was decidedly not blond and not silky.

"Just fill out these forms, honey."

Mrs. Teagle handed me a clipboard.

"And don't forget, lunch is in twenty minutes in the dining hall, which if you recall is here in the lodge, just down the long hallway."

I leaned against a wood-paneled wall, inhaling the sawdusty scent of it. Then I started ticking off answers to the multiple-choice questions.

Are you:

vegetarian?

gluten free?

dairy free?

I'd had a fast-food cheeseburger and a chocolate shake on the drive up to Camden, but on impulse I checked "vegetarian" on my form. Nanny probably would have said I'd done it to be ornery.

I knew laundry service cost extra, so I checked "no" on that, wondering how often I could get away with slipping my clothes into Nanny's laundry bag.

I also checked "no" for the two-day camping trip midway through the session. If anything felt more claustrophobic than staying at Camden for thirty days, it was sleeping in a musty-smelling tent for two of them.

I filled in the last few blanks.

> Food allergies? *Shellfish.*
>
> Animal allergies? *Not unless you count a deep loathing of spiders.*

Then I went to hand my clipboard to Mrs. Teagle. But before she could take it, Nanny swooped over and snatched it out of my hand.

"Ah! Where did you come from?!" I said.

"I was waiting for you," Nanny said, scrutinizing my form. "I thought you might want to sit with me at lunch, it being your first day and all—"

Nanny stopped short and frowned.

"Vegetarian?!" she said.

"I'm . . ." I flailed for a reason for my choice. "I'm just trying something new. Why not?"

"I can think of a few reasons why not," Nanny said. "Starting with your love of fried chicken. And buffalo wings. And pepperoni pizza . . ."

I sighed heavily as Nanny returned to my form.

"Uh-*huh*," she said. "I see you didn't check off anything here, where it asks what class you're taking?"

"I didn't sign up for one," I said with a shrug. "You know, because . . ."

"Because you were going to be my assistant," Nanny provided. "Now you're not. You didn't think you were going to just sit on your fanny all month, did you, young lady?"

"No, of course not!" I said. "I just . . . didn't have a chance to figure out my plan B yet."

"Plan B, eh?" Nanny said. She shuffled through my sheaf of papers until she found the class catalog. She skimmed a fingertip down the list of offerings. "Here's a *B*. Basket weaving. How do you like that? Or, oh, look! They have a class called Bears and Dolls."

"Nan-ny," I said. I didn't roll my eyes because Nanny hates it, almost as much as I hate it when she uses the word "fanny" in public. But in my head, I was *really* rolling my eyes. "It doesn't have to start with *B*."

"I know that," Nanny said. "So just pick one. Looks like pottery and quilting are full, though. They always go the quickest."

"What about your class?" I asked. "Is it full too?"

We found her class listing and saw that there were a couple of openings.

"That's because they're scared of me," Nanny said with an evil grin. "Everyone knows I'm a tough cookie."

"Believe me, Nanny, I *know*," I said. I took the catalog from her. "There are a ton of classes here. I better focus."

"All right," Nanny said. "I'm going to head to my cabin." Camden put all the teachers up in a row of adorable, tiny cabins near the lake. As she opened the door next to the sign-up table, a sweet, green-scented breeze washed over me. The doorway framed a slice of ridiculously blue sky, wildflower-dotted grass, and a stone wall that just begged you to sit on it and write a poem. Before the door swung shut, I heard a snatch of music—a man and a woman, singing an a cappella duet in clear, sweet voices. It was a song I knew (of course), one about a young couple who fall in love and have one blissful month together. Then the boy goes off to the Civil War and dies with his love's name on his lips.

That was what usually happened in these sepia-toned songs— the whole better-to-have-loved-and-lost thing.

I'd always wondered if it were really true—that it was better to have loved and lost than never to have loved at all. I hadn't loved anybody yet. At least, not in the way songwriters and musicians went on about it. Clearly, love—real, feel-it-in-your-bones, swoony love—was just another version of the Joy that I couldn't imagine feeling.

But, I thought as my gaze fell back onto the course catalog, *maybe this is my chance.*

Maybe there was a class here at Camden, hidden in this list among the teddy bears and baskets, that would just feel *right;* the kind of right I'd never felt with music.

I bit my lip as I scanned the list of classes.

Knitting sounded about as exciting as algebra class. Paper Making? Snore. Beading would feel too much like counting down the minutes, bead by clickety bead.

That's when I saw it—the perfect class. In part, this was because nobody would expect me to take it, any more than they'd imagine me becoming a vegetarian.

That must have been why Nanny had skipped right over it, even though it was right there on the first page of the catalog, between Bears & Dolls and Broom Making.

The class had everything I craved. It was as solid and earth-bound as music was ephemeral. And it definitely didn't look like it was going to be boring.

There was space in the teen division of the class. So I checked the box.

Folks, we have a plan B, I thought, feeling a little giddy. *And it's called Blacksmithing.*

Chapter ● Four

There were two vegetarian tables in the dining hall. They were marked by cardboard signs emblazoned with big green *V*s. I thought the signs were mortifying, but as people started to find their places at the big round tables—adults gravitated to one of them, kids to the other—I could tell they were proud of those green *V*s. Even smug.

As I stood next to the table, I bit my lip and placed a hand on my growling stomach. I was the kind of hungry that would *never* be satisfied by a salad.

My yearning for protein was only made worse by the aroma beginning to waft out of the kitchen—salty, earthy, and greasy in the best way.

Fried chicken.

Add hot sauce and you had my favorite food in the world.

I tried not to inhale too deeply. Why torture myself?

This turned out to be a good tactic for another reason. The wonderful aroma from the kitchen was suddenly replaced by another scent—acrid and musky.

What is that?! Burnt seaweed? Charred kale? I thought desperately. *Is that what the vegetarians have to eat?!*

"Hi, roomie!"

Annabelle practically skipped up to the table and smiled at me.

I should have known that someone like Annabelle—with her long, earth-goddess ringlets and her jangly third-world jewelry—would be a vegetarian. And not just an "oh, burgers make me bloated" vegetarian. No, she was definitely going to be one of those "save the world with soy!" types. With her willowy, muscular limbs, she looked like someone who existed on a diet of Swiss chard, quinoa, and yoga.

"Oh, hi," I said, smiling weakly. "So you're a vegetarian? I mean, er, you're a vegetarian too?"

"Of course!" Annabelle said. "I mean, how could you *not* be?!"

Then she launched into another cheery diatribe, her pretty brown eyes sparkling.

". . . and oh my God, the *corn* subsidies . . . and methane gas . . ."

As she went on (and on and on), Annabelle tossed her hair back over her shoulder. Another wave of the smoky smell hit me.

"Um, did you just do that smudging thing in our room?" I asked her.

"Yesssss!" Annabelle said rapturously. "It was incredible, Nell. I wish you'd been there. Talk about a total melding of the spirit, the corporeal, and nature, you know?"

No, I really, really *don't*, I thought.

I must have looked grossed out in addition to confused, because Annabelle lifted a hank of her hair to her nose to give it a sniff.

"I know," she admitted. "I totally reek."

I laughed. "I wasn't going to say anything, but . . ."

"Whoa, what's that smell? Is that burnt sage?"

Annabelle and I both pivoted as a boy approached our table with a wrinkled nose. He was tall and lanky and had sand-colored curls that were just a little too long. His face was tan and freckly and pretty cute.

Annabelle jumped to her feet to face him. I braced myself. Was she going to launch into a lecture about respecting nature (even when nature smelled like overripe shoes)? Maybe she would try to explain that spiritual-corporeal melding thing to *him*.

But instead Annabelle just said, "Um, sorry about that."

Then, after giving the boy a long look, she added, "I'm Annabelle."

She pulled out the chair next to her, inviting the boy to sit down.

He smiled, big and toothy.

"I'm not a vegetarian," he said. "So I don't think I'm supposed to take a spot here. But I wish I could have some of that sage dish

I smell. It reminds me of this butternut squash soup my grandma used to make."

"Oh, so you *like* that scent?" Annabelle asked.

The boy shuddered. "No way! My grandma was a terrible cook. But she was the *best* grandma. That smell makes me miss her."

The boy looked at the ceiling, his eyes a little distant as he clearly lost himself in some happy, if foul-smelling, memory.

When he came back to earth, he seemed to really *see* Annabelle for the first time, instead of just smelling her. His eyes went from murky to riveted. There was another long pause before he seemed to realize that he needed to say something. Anything.

"I'm"—the boy's eyes flickered to the big green *V* on our table—"not a vegetarian."

He'd said this once already. But this time, his voice was full of regret.

Annabelle's shoulders sagged a bit too.

"Well," she said, "I guess you better find a seat then. . . ."

"Owen," the boy said.

He stuck his hand out, and Annabelle looked at it in surprise before giving it a shake.

Owen laughed self-consciously.

"Sorry," he said, "that's another thing my grandma did—made me shake hands whenever I met someone new. I know it's kind of dumb, but I can never seem to lose the habit."

"Oh," Annabelle breathed.

I frowned at her back. Where was her lecture about honoring one's heritage or whatever?

As Owen headed across the dining hall, Annabelle watched him go with eyes as soft as melted chocolate.

"Annabelle," I whispered to her. "Did you hear what the guy said? He's *not a vegetarian.* Don't you have some, y'know, *opinions* about that?"

"Hmmm?" she said vaguely. She was still staring after Owen, still speechless.

I noticed people starting to walk through the dining hall and remembered how meals worked at Camden. A few people from each table fetched big platters of food from the kitchen's service window. Then we ate our meals family-style off handmade crockery dishes and rustic cloth napkins. The idea was that tablemates would get to know one another more easily if they were constantly passing the potatoes.

When I was a kid at Camden, everybody at my table quickly learned that Nanny took her iced tea with a brimming tablespoon of simple syrup, that my little brother lived on bread and butter alone, and that I would hog the drumsticks on fried chicken night.

Today I figured I would hear everyone's vegetarian back-stories. They'd probably talk about caged chickens and overfed pigs and insist that tempeh tasted even *better* than steak. After that, skulking away to eat meat at one of the other tables would become an impossibility, or at least, incredibly awkward.

With a sigh of resignation, I stood up to go fetch one of our table's sad, tasteless, not-meat dishes. But as I turned to head to the kitchen, I narrowly missed crashing into a platter full of gloppy broccoli casserole.

"Ah!" I said, jumping backward.

That's when I saw who was holding the platter.

It was that fiddle student, Jacob.

"Oh, hi," I said. "So you're a vegetarian too."

Jacob cast a fishy glance at the giant green *V* that marked our table.

"Yeah, but what's with the scarlet letter?" he whispered. "I mean, even if it's not red, it's kind of in your face, isn't it?"

"Isn't that the point?" I replied, also whispering. "You know, to make people think twice about eating meat?"

"Well, if that's *your* point . . . ," Jacob said. Now he was directing his fishy look at *me*.

"No!" I blurted. "Not even close. I'm not even veg—"

I clamped my mouth shut just in time. I glanced over Jacob's shoulder at the kitchen.

"There's more food up there, I hope?"

"Yup," Jacob said, putting his casserole onto the table with a thunk. "I'll help you."

As we walked toward the window, he added, "I'm glad it's not just, like, salad, aren't you?"

"I'm going to reserve my answer until after I've tasted the casserole," I said. We reached the kitchen. The vegetarian food was placed on the left edge of the window's counter, far from the platters of crispy chicken parts. I gave the fried meat a longing stare before grabbing some coleslaw and a basket of rolls. Jacob got a bowl of pickled beets and some deviled eggs.

"So, Annabelle's your roommate, right?" Jacob asked as we began wending our way back through the crowded dining hall. At this point, the torturous smell of the chicken was practically tangible. I found myself dodging plumes of the aroma, the way you sidestep travelers in a busy airport.

"Yeah," I answered. "She seems cool. Very . . . informative."

"She kind of reminds me of my older sister," Jacob said. "Last summer, before she started her freshman year at Cornell, she acted like she had a PhD in life. It was like she knew everything about everything. One month in, she started calling my parents and crying about how dumb she felt."

I snorted. "Well, that story's encouraging-slash-discouraging," I said.

"I was going for funny-hyphen-sympathetic," Jacob said, "but I'll take encouraging-slash-discouraging."

Then he smiled at me.

It was such a bright smile, it made me wonder if he'd stopped thinking of me as my grandmother's handbag.

Just before we reached our table, I glanced at the basket of fluffy Parker House rolls in my hand.

"White bread," I reported to Jacob. "I have a feeling Annabelle's not going to like this. She seems like a sprouted wheat kind of girl."

"Maybe it would help if she made a sandwich out of these," Jacob said, holding up his tray of deviled eggs. "If you ask me, mayonnaise makes everything taste better."

"Then you'll feel right at home here," I said. "We definitely have a bit of a mayo fixation in the South."

"I guess it goes with the twang?" Jacob said.

"Well, *that* I wouldn't know," I said. "Since I don't have a twang."

We'd arrived at our table. As he put down his serving dishes and took a seat, Jacob raised one eyebrow at me.

"What?" I demanded, sitting down myself. Only after I scooched my chair in and grabbed my napkin did I realize that I'd plunked myself into the chair next to Jacob's, even though there were three other open seats at the table, including one next to Annabelle. It had felt so natural, I hadn't even thought about it.

Meanwhile, Jacob was still doing that skeptical eyebrow thing.

"Ex*cuse* me, I do *not* have a twang," I said. "Twangs are country, and I've lived in a big city my whole life. Now Nanny—*she's* got the twang."

"Listen, I love Southern accents," Jacob said, unfolding his napkin. "They're kind of musical, aren't they? There's a rhythm to all those extra syllables. And 'y'all.' How awesome is 'y'all'?"

I grinned and rolled my eyes.

"Oh, you Northerners," I teased. "You think we're so quaint, don't you? Never mind that that's kind of *condescending*."

"Well, why do y'all care if y'all don't have a Southern accent?" Jacob said. He gave me another sly glance as he scooped broccoli casserole onto his plate.

This time, I laughed outright.

"Um, that's not exactly how you use it," I said. "Y'all is plural, and *I* am singular."

"But you *do* say y'all?" Jacob asked.

"Of *course* I say y'all," I said with a shrug. "How else am I supposed to talk to people? *Plural* people, that is."

"Up north we say 'you guys,'" Jacob said.

"Well, that's just *wrong*," I said, giggling.

I turned away from him to check out the other vegetarians at our table. Most of them were girls whose style echoed Annabelle's. They had hair that tumbled romantically down their backs and bohemian clothes. Their eyes were alert, almost hungry. I wondered if they were on the lookout for cute boys and if they counted Jacob as one of them.

There was also a younger girl, maybe eleven, but you could tell she wanted us to think she was older. She wore a tank top and cutoff jeans and boots laced up to the knee. She'd chalked an electric-blue stripe into her shiny brown hair. She was listening intently to Annabelle, clearly trying to look like she knew what my roommate was talking about.

". . . and Sadie, don't even get me started on GMOs . . . I mean, really, it's an issue of public *health*, don't you think?"

"Mm-*hmm!*" Sadie said.

The corners of Jacob's mouth were doing that twitchy thing again.

"Annabelle," he said, after taking a big bite of his lunch, "I'm not sure what public health officials would say about this broccoli casserole. There's a *lot* of cheddar going on in there."

"Oh," Annabelle said, her face falling.

She looked like she'd never even used the word "casserole" before, much less eaten one.

"I hate to break it to you, Annabelle," I said, "but you're in the South now. It's not tofu country."

"What about salad?" Annabelle asked desperately. "Is it salad country?"

"Sure, there's gelatin salad, ambrosia salad, Waldorf salad, that coleslaw," Jacob said, motioning to the creamy cabbage that was being passed around the table. "Is that what you mean? You *do* like mayonnaise, don't you?"

As Annabelle's caramel-colored cheeks went a little pale, Jacob laughed.

"Sorry," he said. "My mom's always on a diet. The only mayo in our house is this really gross, fat-free goop. She won't even *buy* cheese. So I'm kind of in love with this lunch."

"Just add it to the list of stuff you adore about this place," I said with a little laugh.

"I *better* love it," Jacob replied. "I bagged about two tons of groceries to pay for it."

"Oh," I whispered.

Faculty families always got their room and board for free, and their class tuition was heavily discounted. So I'd never thought about how expensive it was for the regular students. Now I felt like a jerk.

"So . . ." I searched for another topic and decided, lamely, to go the way of the big green *V.* "What's your reason for being a vegetarian?"

"It's kind of corny," he said. "My family had a potbellied pig for a while."

"No, really?!" I said.

Jacob laughed.

"I know, it's goofy, but my dad's allergic to dogs and cats, and he really wanted us to have a pet," he said. "So he got us this tiny little pig—Sally. She was really cute, I've got to admit. She was white, just like the pig in *Charlotte's Web.*"

"And then what?" I said apprehensively. I could tell this story wasn't going in a good direction. Did Sally end up as their Christmas ham?

"Well, let's just say that if you want your potbellied pig to stay little and cute," Jacob said, "you have to keep her on a very strict diet. Sally got sort of huge. We eventually had to give her to a petting zoo."

"Oh, that's so sad," I said.

"No, it's not," Jacob said matter-of-factly. "Sally's much better off there, and she makes a lot of kids happy. We go visit her every once in a while. And now, none of us can go *near* a ham sandwich. It's been five years since we had Sally, and even my dad hasn't caved. And this is a guy who used to put bacon on *everything*, even ice cream."

"Wow, go Sally," I said with a laugh. "But what about chicken and steak and stuff?"

Jacob shrugged.

"My family eats those things, but I just don't want them anymore. Once you start imagining your pork chop with your pet's face on it, it's pretty easy to make that connection with all meat. It wasn't hard to give it up."

"Oh yeah," I said, even though I seemed to be having trouble forgoing fried chicken for one lousy meal.

I took a bite of pickled beet and tried not to wince at its vinegary sweetness. Then I switched back to the broccoli casserole, chewing miserably. Despite the fact that the casserole was creamy and cheesy and sprinkled with fried onions—not exactly prisoner's rations—I, once again, felt trapped.

If I was home, I complained to myself, *I could be eating whatever I wanted right now. I wouldn't be pretending to be a vegetarian or a blacksmith. I could just be me.*

On the other hand, the me at home was a Finlayson.

I could never escape that.

If I were anything like Jacob, I thought, *I wouldn't want to escape it. I'd be psyched to see my name in liner notes, even if nobody reads liner notes anymore. I'd think of Camden as a gift, not a jail.*

Maybe I'd look forward to hanging out with a bunch of other fiddlers in Nanny's log cabin classroom.

Maybe I'd even be up for a duet with this way-too-earnest vegetarian who had ocean-colored eyes and a thing for mayonnaise and Southern accents.

Maybe . . .

But the fact was, I *wasn't* anything like Jacob. So, I told myself, there wasn't any point in thinking about those things.

Chapter ✺ Five

Until the next day, my first day of class, I'd never actually seen what went on in the dark, mysterious blacksmithing barn. I'd only glimpsed the plumes of black smoke emerging from its stove-pipe chimneys. And I'd heard weighty, rhythmic clangs coming through the grimy, half-open windows. Most of all, I'd seen the blacksmithing students around campus.

They always seemed to sit together in the dining hall (definitely not at a vegetarian table). Their skin always had a sooty, sweaty sheen. Their nails were permanently rimmed in black, and their hair was dusted with ash.

I'd felt like such a badass when I'd signed up for the class. Nothing seemed more different from playing the violin than pounding on molten metal with a very large hammer.

But now, as I slipped through the tall, heavy barn doors, I did not feel tough or brave. I felt small. And for a girl who'd hit five feet seven inches before I even stepped foot in high school, that was a feat.

Everything in the barn seemed to be oversize—the long, thick-legged tables with blackened steel tops, the two massive, blazing forges, the hammers and tongs and other tools dangling from a network of hooks on the wall. The students, too, were big. The kind of big that made you wonder if they'd gone through puberty at age ten. They looked like they all played football when they weren't at Camden—any position that tackled. Either that, or they operated all the heavy machinery on their families' farms. They had meaty arms, enormous, clompy boots, and chins that were mottled with either scruff or soot.

There were no other girls.

When I arrived, the guys were already busy grabbing tools and carving out workstations. They clearly were returning students who knew what they were doing.

"Look who we have here!" said a man who was clearly the instructor. He'd spotted me cowering by the doors. "You must be Annie's granddaughter. When Mrs. Teagle told me you were taking my class, I couldn't believe it. You're going to risk your fiddler's fingers in here?"

Reflexively I curled my hands into fists and slipped them behind my back.

"Um, what?" I said. "I thought losing fingers was more of a woodworking thing."

"Relax," the man said, laughing as he clomped over to me in his big, lace-up boots. "We haven't lost a finger in years! Now as for thumbs . . ."

Then he laughed again. I didn't know if he was joking or just thought losing a thumb was funny. When he held out his hand to shake mine, I couldn't help but take a digit count. No fingers were missing, which eased my mind a little bit.

The fact that his hand was also as big as an oven mitt and covered with scars and burns—well, that ratcheted my nerves right back up.

"I'm Stan," the teacher said. "But all the boys call me Coach."

"Nell," I said, smiling nervously.

"Okay, Nell, seeing as how I'm not letting you anywhere *near* a forge today," he said, "I'm not gonna send you back to your room to change. But tomorrow, I want to see you in close-toed shoes and a shirt that's not so . . ."

Coach seemed at a loss for words as he regarded my tank top, which had several panels of ruffly fabric cascading down the middle of it. It was one of my favorites, because it created the illusion of curves I didn't really have.

"Flammable," he finally said.

I'd actually tried to dress appropriately for the blacksmithing class. I'd paired my tank with denim cutoffs and sturdy walking sandals, and I'd clipped the front bits of my bob away from my face with a couple of glittery hairpins.

I regarded the other students, who were giving me glances

over their piles of heavy tools. Their faces looked either curious or curmudgeonly—it was hard to tell through the flinty gloom. They were all dressed pretty much exactly alike.

"So, the plaid shirts and overalls," I asked Coach, "that's not just fashion?"

"It's not at *all* fashion," Coach said.

"Hey!" called one of the boys, who was pumping air into one of the forges with an old-fashioned bellows. "Speak for yourself, Coach. I think I look *fabulous*."

Deep, throaty laughter rippled around the echoing space, and I joined in.

But the laughter died down quickly when it came time for me to actually join the class. At Coach's instruction, I went to grab some hammers and tongs from the tool wall.

Two of the guys were still there. One of them had a thick unibrow and dark sideburns that never ended. Literally, they snaked across his full cheeks and joined together beneath his nose. He looked about eighteen, but his mustache looked more like thirty.

The other boy had biceps so big they strained the seams of his plaid shirtsleeves.

Their tools made heavy, clanking sounds as they lifted them off the hooks on the wall.

"Hi," I said, giving the two guys a little wave that was so girly, it made me cringe. "Um, I'm Nell."

"Yeah, we heard about you," said hams-for-arms, easily

hoisting a hammer that looked more like a ten-pound dumbbell. He shot a quick glance in Coach's direction, and I wondered if Coach had warned them before I arrived to be nice to the fiddler's granddaughter. "Listen, don't take this the wrong way, but what the heck are you doing here?"

"Yeah, look at that scrawny arm," mustache guy said, pointing at my bare bicep. "You're gonna get hurt."

"I'll be fine," I said, sticking out my chin.

"No, you won't," he replied, and all laughter went out of his black eyes. "You're gonna suck up all of Coach's time because you don't know what you're doing."

I grabbed one of the smaller hammers off the wall and tried not to grunt at its unexpected weight.

"Seriously," I said. "Don't worry about me. You just do your thing."

"Our thing?" Ham-arms said. "Uncensored? Because let me tell you, I just used the word 'heck' for the first time in my life, and I *didn't* like it."

"Yeah, bring it," I blurted. "Swear all you want. I can take it. I don't want things to be any different just because I'm here. And I promise I won't get in your way."

"Uh-huh," muttered mustache guy. "I'll believe that when I see it."

"You'll see it," I said to his very broad back as he headed toward the forge. "Promise."

Here's what I'd learned by the end of my first day as a student blacksmith:

• Mustache boy was named Clint, and ham-for-arms was Joe. The other guys in the plaid crew were named Michael, Jack, and Anthony. Jack was my age, but most of the other boys were seniors in high school. Clint, the oldest, was twenty and worked on his family's farm in South Carolina. (I'd been right about the farm thing.)

• Once I insisted, they did indeed use words a lot stronger than "heck."

• They were strong. Really strong. And in comparison, I was as floppy-armed as Olive Oyl. I know this because that's what the guys called me after they saw me wield a hammer.

• Pounding molten metal? It's excruciating. But also kind of fun.

• Clint had been right—I did get hurt.

I didn't lose a thumb. I only burned the side of my palm when I rested my right hand on a hot anvil.

I snatched my hand away and bit my cheek to keep from crying out. Then I kept the burn hidden at my side until class was over. Luckily, that happened only a few minutes later.

As I headed for the door, Coach clapped me on the shoulder

and said, "Our girl did all right on her first day, didn't she, guys?"

They responded with a grudging grumble of agreement, which only made me feel guilty.

Finally, after promising Coach that I'd show up the next day in boots and a simpler (if not necessarily plaid) top, I dashed back to the dorm to shower. The burn was one big blister by then, and it hurt badly when the warm water ran over it.

I knew exactly what a burn like this needed—antibiotic ointment and a gauze bandage. I'd packed neither. I was sure that Nanny had, though. Grandmas always remembered that kind of practical stuff when they traveled.

But if Nanny learned that I'd singed a single arm hair in my class, let alone gotten a nasty burn, I knew she'd get all mother hen on me and try to make me drop out. I wouldn't be surprised if Coach and the rest of the plaid crew backed her up.

But here was what I'd realized a moment after the burn happened, once the initial searing pain had subsided into a mere painful throb: I really wanted to stay in the blacksmithing class. I didn't know exactly *why* I did, but I did.

Maybe I wanted to fall in love with ironwork. I might even discover that I had a hidden talent for it. That way, nobody could argue that I was destined to be just another fiddling Finlayson.

Maybe I just wanted to get some muscle definition in my noodle arms and learn some new swear words.

Or maybe . . . I had something to prove to myself. I wasn't sure what that something was. I bet if I mentioned it to Annabelle, she'd give me a dozen theories, all in a dialect of psychologese that I couldn't begin to understand.

But of course, I *wasn't* going to discuss my desire to keep blacksmithing with Annabelle, or with anybody else. If I kept my burn a secret, I wouldn't have to fight to stay in the class. I could just show up the next morning and keep on going.

So how was I going to hide this two-inch long blister from everyone? Simple.

I would break into the infirmary.

The infirmary was just a little office in the lodge, located off the long corridor between the lounge and the dining hall. The door didn't even have a proper lock on it. It was just one of those deals with a push-button lock in the interior knob and a hole in the exterior one. Poke around in that hole with a bobby pin— much like the ones that were jabbed into my hair—and *pop*, you were in.

I decided to pop in right after dinner.

I also told myself that I wasn't really doing anything wrong. If I'd gone to the infirmary when it was open, Mrs. Teagle or some other Camden staffer would have happily given me the ointment and bandages. But they'd probably be accompanied by a lecture, a concerned look, and finally: "I'd better discuss this with your grandma."

And that couldn't happen.

My resolve increased as I gingerly got dressed for dinner, sucking in my breath every time a bit of fabric grazed my blister.

I became even more determined as I walked across campus and smelled a hint of steely forge smoke in the air.

In the dining hall, I pretended to be chilled by the air-conditioning and crossed my arms over my middle, hiding the burn against my body.

I'm actually doing the Camden staffers a favor, I told myself as I headed for my table. *Why should anybody go to the trouble of helping me, when I can help myself?*

Chapter ● Six

From the moment I made my decision about the infirmary, everything went perfectly.

At the vegetarian table, I ended up sitting between two of the aloof older girls. They spent the meal talking about college-y stuff and ignoring me, and they definitely didn't notice that I was awkwardly eating with my left hand and hiding my burned right hand beneath the table.

Then there was homemade butterscotch pudding for dessert, which almost made up for the fact that dinner had been yet another casserole, this one involving cream of mushroom soup and green beans. After dessert, everyone cleared out, some for a twilight nature walk and the rest for the nightly sing-along in the great hall upstairs.

All those activities left the corridor outside the infirmary empty. The only other rooms along this hallway were the front office and the kitchen. The office was closed, and when I pressed my ear to the kitchen door, I heard the loud clatter of dishwashing in full swing. It was the perfect moment for a break-in.

Except it's not *really breaking in,* I reminded myself. *I'm just helping myself to something they'd be giving me anyway.*

Then, trying not to feel shifty and evil, I slipped one of the bobby pins out of my hair and poked it into the little hole in the doorknob.

I twisted it. I wiggled it. I jabbed it in and out of the knob several times. But I didn't hear a pop.

Sighing, I squinted into the tiny hole. When I saw nothing but blackness, I tried the bobby pin again, maneuvering it this way and that.

"What are you doing?"

I yelped and straightened up so fast, I knocked my forehead on the doorknob.

Great, I thought. *Injury number two.*

When I saw that it was Jacob who had snuck up behind me, I didn't know whether to be relieved or doubly panicked.

"Um, hi!" I said. "What are you doing here? Don't tell me you want seconds of that green bean casserole."

I gestured lamely at the kitchen door, then laughed even more lamely.

Jacob wasn't fooled for a second. He looked at the little red sign on the door: INFIRMARY, SEE STAFF FOR HELP.

"You're trying to break in," Jacob said, his eyes widening in shock.

"No, see, it's not breaking in. . . ."

I started to explain my logic to him, but I knew if I said it out loud, it would sound . . . not very logical. And not very sane. So I just said, "Listen, it's not how it looks."

"Well, it looks pretty bad," Jacob said. He folded his arms over his chest, and his face went hard. "I bet it's also futile. I seriously doubt you'll find anything stronger than Tylenol in there."

"Wait a minute," I gasped. "Do you think I'm here for *drugs*? Are you crazy?"

Jacob looked confused.

"Well, why else does someone break into an infirmary?"

I held up my right hand, showing him the raw, blistery welt on the edge of my palm. He winced.

"I need *Neosporin*," I blurted. "And some super-duper Band-Aids."

"What happened?" Jacob asked. I dropped my gross hand to my side so he would stop staring at it.

"It's nothing," I said roughly. "I just had a little accident in blacksmithing class."

"And they didn't have a first-aid kit in the barn?" Jacob demanded. "I mean, that kind of thing must happen all the time."

"I don't know if they have a first-aid kit," I said. "I didn't ask."

"Why not?"

"Jacob, I'm *supposed* to be assisting in your fiddle class," I said. "That's the whole reason my family shipped me out here against my will."

"And you're not supposed to be a blacksmith?" Jacob asked.

"I'm sure that's what Nanny thinks," I said. "And I *know* that's what every guy in my class thinks. Probably the teacher, too."

"I think Annabelle would call that sexist," Jacob said. His face had lost its accusatory hardness. It was even warming into what looked like a pre-smile.

"I don't think so, actually," I said truthfully. "I think they'd like me just fine if I were built like Rosie the Riveter instead of Olive Oyl, or if I could teach them a swear word they'd never heard of. But trust me, these guys know a *huge* number of swear words. I can't compete."

"So your thinking is, all they need to kick you out of the class is proof that you're not up to the challenge?"

I slumped against the hallway wall and nodded.

"But you *want* to stay in the class," Jacob went on, cocking his head and raising his eyebrows.

"Why are you so surprised?" I said.

Now it was Jacob's turn to look squirmy. He shrugged.

I straightened myself up and squinted at him.

"Oh, I get it," I said. "*You* think I'm a quitter. Just because I didn't want to be Nanny's fiddle assistant."

"No . . . ," Jacob trailed off. He wouldn't meet my eyes.

"Listen, Jacob," I said. "I'm not *quitting* fiddle. It's not *mine* to quit. Do you get what I mean?"

"But it *is* yours," Jacob insisted. "You're a Finlayson. Don't you know how lucky that makes you?"

"Now you sound just like my grandmother!" I sputtered.

Jacob started to retort, but then closed his mouth and looked sheepish.

"Um, you're right," he said. "Your grandma is, well, she really gets into your head."

"What you're saying is she's a brute," I said with a grin. "How did she torture you guys today? Did she make you do scales until you cried?"

Jacob held up his left hand.

"I literally got a cramp in my pinkie," he said. "That's never happened to me before."

"Yeah, Nanny always does that on day one," I said. "It's hazing. Students' pain amuses her."

Jacob laughed, but then gestured to my hand.

"Does that hurt a lot?" he asked.

I shrugged. My hand was throbbing, but he didn't need to know that.

Jacob glanced at the doorknob.

"Maybe that's why you're having trouble popping that lock," he said thoughtfully.

"It was a dumb idea," I sighed. "I mean, I'm clearly going to get kicked out of the class one way or another. I might as well just go get Mrs. Teagle and tell her what happened."

With my good hand, I started to shove my bobby pin into the pocket of my cutoffs. But Jacob stopped me by grabbing my elbow.

"Wait," he said.

I wouldn't say I *gasped* when Jacob grasped my arm. But I definitely inhaled sharply. Jacob's cool, dry hand on my skin felt good—a kind of good that I'd never felt before. The pressure of his fingers was somehow strong and whispery all at once. It made the throbbing in my hand whoosh its way into my chest.

When he pulled his hand away, it left a tingling imprint on my skin. The tingle seemed to travel to my brain, blanketing it in fuzz. That must have been why I didn't react when Jacob took the bobby pin out of my hand and went to work on the doorknob himself.

I should have stopped him, of course.

I could have pointed out that a girl who couldn't even pick a lock had no business in a blacksmith shop anyway.

I might have channeled Annabelle and told Jacob not to treat me like a damsel in distress.

But instead I just stood there, feeling my arm tingle and staring at him. As he bent over the doorknob, Jacob's T-shirt clung to his back, which had just the right ratio of skinniness to muscle. A lock of his glossy dark hair flopped over his forehead in a perfect swoop.

What with the swooping, the tingling, and the staring, I sort of forgot how wrong this was. This boy was breaking into the Winnie J. Camden infirmary for *me*.

Then I heard the unmistakable sound of Mrs. Teagle's voice. And very quickly, I *did* remember how wrong this was.

Her voice, warbling a few lines of a hymn, was coming from the dining hall, and it was getting louder. Any second now, she would turn the corner and spot us.

"Jacob!" I whisper-shrieked.

Pop!

Jacob turned the knob and the door creaked slowly open. But slowly *anything* wouldn't do, not when we were milliseconds from being caught.

I crouched low and *sprang* at Jacob. Together we tumbled into the moonlit infirmary. Jacob landed on his side with an "*Oof.*" And me?

I landed right on top of him with such momentum that I tipped him over onto his back. When we finally stopped moving, a few things became instantly clear.

(1) My body was stretched out on top of Jacob's. That meant our noses were touching. Our lips were within an inch of each other. And all sorts of other body parts were touching too.

(2) I'd hit Jacob so hard that I'd knocked the breath out of him. So while he could stare at me in shock, he couldn't quite form words. This turned out to be a lucky thing, because . . .

(3) I could hear the *squeak, squeak, squeak* of Mrs. Teagle's practical, rubber-soled shoes coming down the hallway.

I sprang off Jacob with catlike coordination. Clearly, complete mortification plus mortal terror had given me superhuman powers.

I skittered back to the door, then made myself screech to a

halt before I smoothly but swiftly swung it closed. The last bit was the hardest—painstakingly untwisting the doorknob so it didn't click into place.

I did a pretty good job keeping this maneuver quiet.

But was it *silent*?

Not even close.

Mrs. Teagle's shoes stopped squeaking. She had paused, I was almost certain, just outside the door.

I looked around wildly for a place to hide. But the infirmary was lined with open shelves. There wasn't a single closet. There weren't even curtains on the small window. We had no cover whatsoever.

Our only option was an almost-empty corner behind the door. This corner was so tight, there was no room to store anything there except a couple of brooms and an umbrella.

I made like a broom and wedged myself into the corner, motioning for Jacob to join me. He was still sitting on the floor, still out of breath. He gaped at me, gave his head a quick shake, and mouthed, *Impossible*.

But then the doorknob made a quiet clickety sound. It was the sound of Mrs. Teagle placing her hand on the knob and turning.

He had no choice. Jacob scrambled to his feet and, with a single leap, landed in the corner with me.

The door opened.

I tipped my head back, sucked in my stomach, and stood on my tiptoes—anything to somehow make myself take up less space.

With no wall left to melt into, Jacob pressed back into *me*. Hard.

This time, I couldn't spring away from him like a spooked cat. I could only stand there and feel his back, hard and warm, pressing against my torso. I was also aware of his taut legs covering mine. And of his forearms, grazing my hips.

Most of all, I could smell Jacob. He smelled like sun-warmed grass, with a tangy hint of sweat and a bolder dash of citrusy deodorant. He pretty much smelled better than anything I've ever smelled before, even fried chicken.

I closed my eyes, awash in that scent and the exquisite discomfort of him squashing me. Somewhere in that haze, I remembered to pray for it all to be over; for Mrs. Teagle to miss us and move on.

It was definitely a long shot. Even with all that willful flattening, there was only room for the door to open halfway. If Mrs. Teagle pushed it any farther, it would knock into us. We were a human doorstop.

I felt Jacob tense from head to toe. I bit my lip and held my breath.

By some miracle, the door stopped just before it connected with Jacob's nose. He jerked his head backward, lightly bonking me on my forehead.

Click.

The dusky room suddenly filled with fluorescent light.

"Hmmm," Mrs. Teagle murmured on the other side of the door. She paused for a long, *long* moment, then whispered, "Ears playing tricks on me."

Click went the light back off.

Swoosh went the door—closed again.

Jacob took a quick step out of the corner and whirled to stare at me.

"Did we seriously just get away with that?" he whispered.

Equally dumbfounded, I grinned and nodded.

At least, I tried to nod. But I found that I couldn't. A sudden pain on the back of my head made me yelp.

"My hair!" I whispered. "It's stuck!"

I'd been so wedged into the corner that a hank of my hair had clearly snaked between the open door and its frame. When Mrs. Teagle had closed it, she'd inadvertently trapped me.

Jacob held a finger in the air. *Wait a minute.*

Stupidly, I tried to nod again, then gritted my teeth as my hair got another painful yank. Of course, Jacob was right. Only once Mrs. Teagle had left the hallway could we open the door and release me.

We waited a long beat during which even breathing seemed to pull at my scalp.

Finally Jacob reached for the knob.

But before he could turn it, Mrs. Teagle's voice rang out from the hallway.

"What is this?"

I felt a tug on my hair. Clearly, Mrs. Teagle had spotted it tufting through the door frame.

The door swooped open, releasing me and banging into me all at once.

"Ow!" I groaned as light flooded the room once again.

"*What* is going on in here?"

Mrs. Teagle's throaty voice still reminded me of a mama robin's. But now she was a bird in a rage, flappy and cawing.

Jacob's face went pale, and red splotches burst out on his neck.

That's when I realized just how bad this looked. It looked bad enough to get us both kicked out of Camden. I couldn't let that happen to Jacob. He was so excited to study with Nanny, and he'd only gotten one day with her.

"Mrs. Teagle, wait!" I cried, jumping out from behind the door. "This isn't Jacob's fault."

"I don't see how that's possible, young lady," Mrs. Teagle said. "He's trespassing as much as you are."

"But Jacob is only here for me!" I said, desperately. To prove it, I thrust my oozy hand toward Mrs. Teagle's face. "I got burned today in blacksmithing class. I didn't want anyone to know, so I just thought I'd sneak in here and help myself to some bandages and stuff."

"Well, that's the silliest thing I ever heard!" Mrs. Teagle sputtered.

"Not if you know how badly Nell wants to learn blacksmithing," Jacob piped up. "She doesn't want her grandma or Coach to make her quit just because she made a mistake."

I shot him a grateful glance, but Mrs. Teagle was clearly less moved than I was by Jacob's little speech.

"Burning yourself is a forgivable mistake," she said. She pointed dramatically at the open door. "*That* is not."

"I promise, Mrs. Teagle," I said. "I just wanted a little Neosporin."

Mrs. Teagle squinted at me and then at Jacob. As she looked back at me, I saw something shift and soften in her eyes.

"Oh," she said. "Oh, I see."

Jacob and I glanced at each other. *What* did she see?

Mrs. Teagle actually smiled a little bit as she closed the door. Then she motioned for me to sit on the infirmary's examining table while she bustled around, gathering medical supplies from drawers and cabinets. While Jacob hovered nervously by the wall, Mrs. Teagle grabbed my arm and started swabbing at my burn with disinfectant.

"Oooofffff!" I grunted in pain. Strangely, this seemed to make Mrs. Teagle even more cheery.

"You know, I was a nurse before I had my children," she chirped. "Even though they're all grown now, I still remember all my training."

She squirted some ointment onto my burn, slapped on some gauze, and wrapped my hand in medical tape. Then, after piling more bandages and ointment packets into my arms, Mrs. Teagle shooed me and Jacob out of the infirmary like a farmwife herding her backyard chickens.

"Thanks so much, Mrs. Teagle," I said. "I promise, nothing like this will ever happen again."

"Absolutely," Jacob agreed.

"Oh, I know that, sweethearts," Mrs. Teagle said with a smile. "But we're not finished yet. Come with me."

Jacob and I exchanged another glance as Mrs. Teagle led us a few steps down the hallway and into the kitchen. A trio of staffers in damp white aprons were scrubbing at countertops and putting tools away with a loud clatter. Mrs. Teagle had so quickly reverted to her sweet, mama-bird self that for a delusional instant, I thought she was going to give us milk and cookies.

"I reckon you'll need about three days for that burn to heal enough," Mrs. Teagle said, crossing her arms over her bosom and grinning at us. "Then you can both start."

"Start . . . what?" Jacob asked.

Mrs. Teagle pointed at the industrial-size sink, which was brimming with dirty pots and pans. Next to it was a short stack of soiled dinner plates. It was only short because tray after tray of the plates had already been sent through a loudly churning dishwasher. One of the workers was stacking the hot plates onto a cart, her face pink and sweaty from the steam.

"Betty," Mrs. Teagle called, "I got you some little elves to help. They'll do the after-dinner shift starting Thursday, all right? That'll free you up to make those scones you've been nagging me about. They'll be here for three days."

As Ms. Betty grinned and gave us all a thumbs-up, Mrs. Teagle turned to me and Jacob.

"Me, I like a classic old biscuit, but Betty watched too much Food Network over the winter, and she's gotten all fancy on us," she said. Then, without breaking her sweet smile, she added,

"I trust you'll take this punishment over telling your Nanny or Coach what *really* happened?"

"Yes, ma'am," I said. "But Mrs. Teagle, you really shouldn't punish Jacob, too. This is all my fault."

"No, no," Jacob jumped in to say. "I did pop the lock. I deserve this just as much."

I raised my eyebrows at Jacob. Why wouldn't he let me thank him—and apologize to him—by taking the fall by myself?

"And now, won't you join me for the sing-along?" Mrs. Teagle said.

It wasn't a question. We followed her out of the kitchen and up the stairs to the great hall, a lofted room whose exposed beams and slanting ceiling bounced notes around better than any recording studio.

Before I knew it, Mrs. Teagle had thrust a weathered binder full of sheet music into my hands and ushered me into the soprano section. I sat down next to the girl I'd seen the day before, the one who was taking the canning class. She smiled at me and showed me what page to turn to in the binder. As she did, I couldn't help but notice a bandage on her inner arm, a few inches above her wrist.

"Kitchen burn?" I whispered, pointing to her swatch of gauze. Then I held up my hand. "Mine's from blacksmithing."

"Awesome," the girl said with a grin. "It's a badge of honor, right?"

Not hardly, I thought, feeling a fresh wave of guilt wash over me. I craned my neck, searching for Jacob among the tenors.

I wanted to lock eyes with him so I could telegraph how sorry I was.

Or maybe I just wanted to get one more glimpse of his eyes' deep, dark blue.

But Jacob was hidden in the back of the tenor section, and I couldn't see him. My hand had also started to throb again, and I suddenly felt limp with fatigue.

The path of least resistance?

Singing.

The song was "Darling Clementine," which of course I knew. I slipped into the soprano harmony without even thinking about it.

> *"Ruby lips above the water,*
> *Blowing bubbles, soft and fine,*
> *But, alas, I was no swimmer,*
> *So I lost my Clementine."*

The usual doom and gloom of the song didn't bother me that much this time. The familiarity of the tune was even a little comforting, like the same twisty stretch I did every morning of my life, no matter what bed I was sleeping in.

That, of course, was karma's cue to make me *un*comfortable.

"All right, folks," announced the song leader, who peered at us through glasses perched at the end of his nose. "Let's mix it up a little. You're not a *real* harmonizer unless you can do it next to someone singing a different part. So go on. I want tenors with altos, sopranos with basses, altos with sopranos, whatever crazy combo you can come up with."

Everybody laughed and murmured as they began to shuffle around the room.

I bit my lip and looked around. Over in the altos, I spotted both Nanny and Annabelle. But something made me skirt them and head over to guys' side of the room.

Specifically, to the tenors.

The chair next to Jacob was empty, and I slipped into it. We barely had time to glance at each other before the leader called out, "Page forty-six!" and blew into a little pitch pipe to give us our starting notes.

And then we were singing.

Everybody in the room sang, of course, but it felt to me like just the two of us—me and Jacob.

His voice, like mine, wasn't the strongest. He was on the low end of tenor, and sometimes he had to strain for the high notes. My voice was a little reedy and scratchy.

But that didn't matter. It also didn't matter that I was too shy to meet his eyes, and that he was white-knuckling the songbook. We still hit just the right notes, our voices swirling together as easily as sugar and soft butter on their way to becoming cake.

Even I was a little excited by this. Perfect harmonizing like that doesn't usually happen on the first try, much less in the midst of dozens of other voices.

When we hit the last stanza, I snuck a glance Jacob's way.

He seemed to feel my gaze and looked at me. Then he lifted one corner of his mouth in a grudging smile.

I didn't have to say sorry or thank you. I didn't have to say anything at all. The music said those things for me, and Jacob forgave me.

Chapter ✦ Seven

By Thursday, my burn had gone from a raw, red blister to a peeling pink welt that was tender, but not unbearable.

Maybe this was because I had other aches and pains to contend with. Arm, back, and neck muscles that I'd never known I had were sore. Several strands of my hair had been singed into wiry crisps before Coach told me to lay off the hair products. And the soles of my feet were tired after standing at the anvil for hours at a time.

At least, unlike my classmate Anthony, I still had my eyebrows. I'd also developed a tiny bit of blacksmith pride. I looked like a real smith (well, a miniature version of one) in knee-length cargo shorts, a pair of old, red Doc Martens, and a ribbed tank top fitted enough to stay clear of fire or swinging hammers.

I'd learned a ton of blacksmithing basics. I now knew the difference between a ball-peen hammer and a cross-peen one. I'd learned to get a fire to that magical temperature that wouldn't leave my iron cold and stiff, but wouldn't turn it into a molten puddle, either.

Most of all, I'd started hammering out some iron knick-knacks.

Ugly, misshapen, unusable knickknacks, but hey, it was a start.

A lot of others at the vegetarian table were in the same place as me—that giddy, messy, just-starting-to-get-something phase. At least, that was what I gathered when I slumped into the dining hall on Thursday night.

Marnie and Isabelle, two college girls who were taking quilting together, showed us the needle injuries on their fingertips.

"I swear, I lost a pint of blood!" Isabelle said proudly.

Ronnie, who was working in Camden's organic garden and chicken coop, was telling Jacob, "I never knew compost could be so *fascinating*!"

As he nodded at Ronnie, Jacob put his fist beneath his chin so that his knuckles rested right beneath his nostrils. It was a polite but clear (to me, anyway) odor-blocking move.

I was sitting next to Annabelle and whispered to her, "Poor Jacob. Does Ronnie have no idea that compost might be fascinating but it's also *stinky*?"

"Oh, I'm no one to talk," Annabelle said, pushing a corkscrew out of her tired eyes. Her fingers were wrinkly after a day smushing around wet clay. A streak of the stuff was crusted near her hairline. "I probably smell like a root cellar."

I gave her a sniff.

"A little," I admitted. "But that's not a bad smell. I mean, who doesn't like a sweet potato? Speaking of which . . ."

Across the table, I made eye contact with Jacob, then smiled and motioned to the bowl of mashed potatoes near his plate.

I expected him to smile back as he passed the food my way.

Because we'd exchanged a *lot* of shy smiles ever since that harmonious sing-along.

There'd also been many sidelong glances.

And him saying, "How's your burn?"

And me asking, "How was fiddle class today?"

But somehow, it felt like we were doing more than exchanging polite pleasantries.

Maybe it was because we shared secrets. We'd committed a criminal act together and been sentenced to covert kitchen duty.

Maybe there was a *different* kind of connection between us. An attraction.

Or maybe, I thought now as Jacob passed the bowl without a single look at me, much less a smile, *I imagined it all.*

I frowned as the potatoes reached me. I also realized I didn't actually want any. I scooped out a tiny dollop, just for show. Then I turned to Annabelle to ask her if she thought Jacob was being weird.

In the next instant, I stopped myself.

Is he being weird? What's he thinking? Should I ask—?Does he—?

Those were the kinds of questions a girl asks about a boy she's infatuated with.

And of course, I wasn't infatuated with Jacob.

Was I?

I shot another quick glance Jacob's way. He looked a little pale, especially next to Ronnie, who already had the burnished skin and peeling nose of a real farmer. Jacob was shoveling in his salad and potatoes, but he did it joylessly, like he barely tasted his food. Even his hair was a little saggy and dull.

Yet somehow, all this moroseness made him look cuter than ever.

I decided I *would* ask Annabelle what she thought. But before I could say anything, she was whispering to me.

"So you say I smell like a sweet potato," she said. "Do you think maybe *Owen* likes sweet potatoes?" I was so absorbed in Jacob hypotheticals that it took me a moment to figure out who she was talking about.

"Owen?" I asked. "Oh, *Owen!*"

I craned my neck to see if I could spot him. There he was. Talking and laughing and gesturing with a forkful of delicious-looking meat loaf. "What I think he likes about *what*?"

"Do you think he likes sweet potatoes?"

I looked at Annabelle in confusion.

"Does he like . . . ," I began. Then I started to laugh. "Annabelle, I think the question you really want to ask is, does he like *you*?"

Annabelle shrugged and looked sheepish.

Feeling kind of happy to have a diversion from my Jacob confusion, I peered over at Owen again.

"Why don't you just . . . ask him?" I said. "Isn't that exactly the kind of thing you said you'd do at Camden? Just *going* for the guy is a great example of sucking the marrow out of life, isn't it? *And* you'll be rejecting traditional gender roles. Bonus!"

Annabelle blinked at me.

"Yes," she said. "You're absolutely right."

"So . . ."

I nodded in Owen's direction.

"So," Annabelle sputtered, "that doesn't mean I'm going to *do* it."

I stared at her for a flabbergasted moment before I started laughing.

"Stop!" Annabelle ordered me. But her lips were twitching as she said it, and before I knew it, she was cackling along with me.

"What's so funny, you guys?" asked Sadie. Our eleven-year-old tablemate was sitting next to me on the other side. Today she wore a crisply ironed sleeveless shirt and a red-and-white-checked miniskirt. She looked more like a cute 1950s housewife than a middle schooler.

Annabelle and I looked at each other. We knew the cruelest thing we could say to Sadie was, "You wouldn't understand."

So I just said, "We're talking about how ideas are the easy part, action is the hard part."

"Especially," Annabelle said, "when it comes to boys."

"Oh, booooooys," Sadie said, nodding sagely. "I get it."

"You do?" I said, raising my eyebrows.

Sadie gave the rest of the table a shifty look to make sure nobody was listening.

"Not really," she admitted. "Mostly, I pretty much think boys are aliens."

I laughed.

"I kind of think the same thing," I whispered.

Encouraged by this, Sadie wrinkled her nose. "I mean, aren't they gross?"

"Eh, I was thinking more foreign and mysterious," I said, "rather than green and slimy."

"Oh," Sadie said. She gave me a disapproving look before returning her attention to her dinner.

I glanced at the big clock on the dining room wall. Like everything else at Camden, it was folksy and old. The minute hand shuddered every time it moved. And with every shudder, I was that much closer to dishwashing duty with one of those alien boys.

Jacob was especially foreign and mysterious. He was all earnest fanboy one moment, a burglar the next. And then there were those *smiles* he was always shooting at me. Surely they meant something. But it was just as possible they meant nothing. Who could tell?!

It was much easier to think about some other girl and boy before I snuck off to the kitchen.

So I whispered in Annabelle's ear. "You *could* just say hi to him after dinner, you know."

"Of course I could," she replied. "But *then* what?"

"Annabelle," I said. "I know I've only known you for five days, but in those five days, you've *never* been at a loss for words once. I mean, not even in your sleep. "

It was true. The second night in our cozy little room, I'd woken at two a.m. to hear Annabelle murmuring, "But is it *organic?*"

"Don't overthink it. Just do it. You can tell me how it goes later," I said by way of good-bye.

I grabbed my dishes and slipped away before she could ask where I was going, especially with Jacob MacEvoy just a couple of steps behind me.

Chapter ☕ Eight

Jacob was still quiet when we reported to the kitchen, but that was okay—Ms. Betty did all the talking for us.

"Finally, you're here!" she said.

"Oh, are we late?" I cried. "Supper just ended."

"For you, maybe," Ms. Betty said. She pointed at a big steel table beneath the service window. It was stacked high with trays, plates, and serving bowls.

"Those start showing up about fifteen minutes into the meal," Ms. Betty said. "And *that's* when our shift starts."

We nodded as Ms. Betty started rattling off instructions.

"Get yourselves some aprons, babies. You're going to get wet. And dirty."

She pointed us toward a supply closet. "Grab a couple baseball caps too. This is a kitchen, you keep your heads covered. Now come meet your new best friend, Hobart."

Hobart, it turned out, was the dishwasher—a hulking, belching metal box with two big levers that operated entry and exit doors.

Our job, Ms. Betty explained, would be to arrange the dishes in huge plastic trays with perforated bottoms, spray them off with a nozzle that bounced at the end of a long, silvery hose, then shove the trays into the Hobart one at a time.

The spitting, chugging box did its washing work in only a few minutes. Then it was time to lever open the exit door, unleashing a massive cloud of steam. Ms. Betty told us to use big black gloves to pull out the scalding tray, then stack the clean dishes on a rolling cart for the next morning.

"Got it?" Ms. Betty barked after she'd explained all this to us. We nodded numbly.

"Now, Hobart here's got a few quirks," Ms. Betty said. "He likes to jam up if you put in too many dishes. If you let the detergent get too low, his motor'll burn out and then you're washing all these dishes by hand. The conveyer belt'll freeze if you push the tray in too fast *or* too slow."

"Are you sure you trust us with, um, Hobart?" I said. "I'm scared we're going to break him."

Ms. Betty just laughed.

"No worries!" she said. "He's a hulk. You *can't* break him, not completely anyway. And I'll tell you a secret. When in doubt, give him a wallop. It works nine times out of ten."

To demonstrate, Ms. Betty gave Hobart a big, open-palmed whack, which seemed to make its (his?) *swish-swash-churn* noises step up their rhythm a bit.

Once we (sort of) knew what to do, Ms. Betty retreated to the food prep part of the kitchen, where one of the other staffers, Ms. Eleanor, was mopping the floor. The last worker, Ms. Loretta, was in the back, stocking the walk-in fridge.

Ms. Betty pulled out a massive crockery bowl and announced to all of us, "*I* am going to make pecan praline scones. They are going to be dee-lectable, and Teagle is going to be eating her words! And my scones!"

While she turned on the radio and began measuring out massive amounts of flour, Jacob and I cautiously approached the now-looming tower of dishes. Jacob used one of the rolling carts to transport them from the window to the rinsing area, where I stacked them on a tray and hosed them down.

Okay, *stacked* might be a generous term.

The truth was, I quickly got overwhelmed by the teetering stacks of dishes and just started grabbing whatever was closest. Bowls, mugs, glasses, plates—I frantically scraped them into a compost barrel, then wedged them into their tray as quickly as I could. I held my breath as I shoved the whole business into the Hobart, which I fully expected to hack and cough and shudder to a halt.

But somehow, it didn't. So I kept on loading and shoving, loading and shoving, until—

"Um, Nell?"

Jacob had wandered over from the receiving end of the Hobart, looking pink and damp. The hair peeking out from beneath his baseball cap had waved up in the steam, and his glasses were smudged.

It was almost annoying how good a person could look under such uglifying conditions.

"I wonder if, y'know, *organizing* the dishes would make it easier," he said. "Say, plates with plates? Bowls with bowls?"

"No time!" I blurted. I grabbed the sprayer and hosed down the tray. I might have also splattered the counter, my apron, and one of my shoes. "There's too many."

"No, really," Jacob said. "It's easy. I'll help."

He quickly whisked the leftovers off some dinner plates and assembled them into a neat stack on the stainless-steel counter. Then he carefully pushed the stack toward me the way you leave food on a stump for a wild rabbit.

"Oh, all right," I said. I grabbed the top four plates on the stack, cradled them to my chest, then began to prop them between the stubby plastic prongs on the next tray.

"Okaaaay," Jacob said dubiously.

"What?!" I demanded. "Look, they're lined up like little soldiers, just like you wanted."

"But it could be so much faster if you just—"

Jacob paused and exhaled heavily. "Okay, you're right," he said. "I'm ridiculously type A."

"*And* a stalker," I reminded him. "Let's not forget that."

"Fine, fine," he sputtered with a mock glower. "You can put it on a sign. I'll wear it around my neck, right next to my big green *V, if* you'll just let me stack that tray."

"Hey, stack away," I said, holding up my hands and taking a step backward. "But I'm telling you, it's not going to be any faster."

Jacob stared down the dishwashing tray for a split second before he began shuffling the dinner plates from his left hand to his right. He used his right hand to plunk the plate into a neat, upright position.

Pass, prop, pass, prop.

In about fifteen seconds, the plates were lined up, but there was still an empty section on the tray. Jacob filled it with glasses, each a perfect fit until only a little gap was left in the corner. For that, Jacob swept up a bouquet of spoons and plunked them into the crevice. He carefully sprayed the whole thing down in precise horizontal strokes. Then he shoved the tray into the Hobart and pumped his fist.

"I knew bagging all those groceries would pay off someday," he said.

"You're like a Hobart savant!" I said.

Jacob laughed, but as he began filling the next tray, I sensed his dinnertime gloom returning. I could see it in his shoulders, which were just a little too high and tense; in his Adam's apple, bobbing over and over; in the angle of his head, which was a notch lower than it needed to be.

"Jacob?" I asked.

Somehow, I didn't need to say anything else.

"It's just . . . I didn't come here to become a *dishwashing* prodigy," Jacob said.

"Something happened in class today," I said. "Didn't it?"

"Eh, it's nothing," Jacob said. "Only that apparently I've been bowing incorrectly my entire life."

"Oh, you have not!" I scoffed. "Fiddling is really different from classical violin, you know. You just have to get the hang of it. It's not a big deal, trust me."

"Easy for you to say," Jacob muttered.

He was right. I'd never thought twice about my bow hold. Or my fingering. Or any number of musical techniques. I just *played* because I literally always had.

I knew saying any of this to Jacob would only make me look cluelessly entitled, and make him feel worse.

And besides, the Hobart was beeping, clamoring for me to pull out the tray.

I went to the other side of the washer and pulled the lever that raised the little garage door. Then I plunged my left arm into the steam and hooked the tray with my fingertips.

"Nell!"

Jacob's shout had barely reached me when suddenly *he* reached me. He dove for my arm and snatched my hand out of the Hobart. Then, scowling, he flipped my hand over so it rested in his palm.

"What's wrong?" I blurted.

Except my words didn't come out loud and irate, the way

blurting usually does. My voice had gone reedy and breathless.

Jacob's hands were damp and pruney. His grip was too tight. And yet, his touch still made me speak in the voice of Snow White.

Without answering my question, Jacob peered at my fingertips.

"What's wrong?" I repeated. My voice had gone back to normal, now that it was clear that Jacob *hadn't* grabbed my hand in a fit of passion.

"Nothing," Jacob said, shaking his head in incredulity. "Your hand is totally fine, even though Ms. Betty said you'll get steam burns if you don't wear those to unload the Hobart."

He pointed at the thick, black rubber gloves that were wadded up near the Hobart's exit door.

"Oh yeah," I said. I glanced over my shoulder at Ms. Betty. I hoped she hadn't seen my gaffe. "I guess this is just another example of me being hopelessly type B to your A."

"Yeah, but you're not hurt," Jacob marveled. He poked at the tip of my left index finger. "Wow!" he said. "I guess *that's* why."

"Excuse me?" I pulled my hand away from him and hid it behind my back.

"Your calluses are almost as gnarly as your grandma's," Jacob said.

"Thanks a lot," I protested.

"No, that's a compliment!" Jacob assured me. "Those calluses are awesome. But how do you still have them? I thought you didn't play anymore."

I looked at him as if he'd just spoken to me in Japanese.

"Are you kidding? How could I get away with that?"

Jacob looked pointedly at my right hand—the one I'd burned on the anvil.

"Hello?" he said. "Didn't you trade in your bow for a sledge-hammer?"

"I mostly use a cross-peen hammer," I said, "and please. That's only for this month at Camden. Back home, I can't get away with not playing. I tour with my family on weekends and school breaks. We record. We have these endless jams on our front porch and—"

Jacob looked a little shifty-eyed as I ticked off all my fiddle-playing duties.

"—and you know all these things already, don't you?" I said.

"It's on your grandma's Wikipedia page," Jacob protested. "Right there for the whole world to see. I'm not a stalker, I swear!"

While I tried not to laugh, Jacob turned to grab some clean dishes from the still-steaming rack.

The "still-steaming" part proved problematic for his glasses. Immediately, they fogged up.

"Whoa!" he muttered. Completely blind, he stumbled a few steps backward, knocking right into a dirty dish cart. A bowl full of flatware tumbled noisily to the floor.

Clearly mortified, Jacob looked in my general direction, with his glasses still misted over and his baseball hat askew.

That's when the laugh I'd been biting back burst forth.

Jacob swiped off his glasses and stared at the forks and spoons scattered across the tile floor.

I held my breath and tried to stop laughing, which, of course, only made me laugh louder.

"I'm sorry," I gasped. "I'm just picturing a Three Stooges movie."

"But there're only two of us," Jacob said.

At once, both of us looked over at Ms. Betty, who at that moment was scraping big hunks of sticky dough off her hands and muttering, "This never happens when I make biscuits. Durn Brits!"

"Bwa, ha, ha!"

Now it was *both* of us cackling, him bent over at the waist and me stumbling around as I scooped spoons off the floor.

Then the Hobart beeped again, attracting Ms. Betty's attention.

"Listen, you two," she called over to us. "Cute don't get the dishes done."

I cringed in embarrassment and glanced at Jacob. He, too, quickly stopped laughing.

"All right," I said. "Clearly we have a division of labor. You load."

"And you, Leatherhands, unload," Jacob said, grinning as he returned to his side of the Hobart.

"Just for that," I said, "I'm not going to tell you my idea."

"About what?" Jacob asked, leaning backward so he could see me around the dishwasher.

"About that bowing problem you're having," I said lightly as

I stacked up clean plates. "I bet Nanny told you to bend the bone between your wrist and elbow, didn't she?"

"*Yes!*" Jacob cried. "I mean, seriously? That's like telling someone to breathe through their eyelids."

"What, you can't breathe through your eyelids?" I said. "How do you do the breast stroke?"

Even though I was busy scooping forks into a metal canister, I could just *feel* Jacob gaping at me.

"*Kidding!*" I yelled over my shoulder. "C'mon, I may have E.T. fingers, but I'm not a *complete* mutant."

Then Jacob said something, a phrase that got swept away by the *chug, chug, chug* of the Hobart and the noisy spray of the water. I couldn't discern the words, but something about the tone made me catch my breath.

It made my hands, grasping a handful of serving spoons, suddenly feel weak and shaky.

It made me turn around to look at Jacob.

I didn't need to hear his words to know that he had just paid me a compliment.

The sudden blotches on his neck and the way his eyes couldn't bear to meet mine? Well, that confirmed it.

But I was too shy to ask him what he'd said.

And he was clearly too embarrassed to repeat it.

The next thing I knew, it was me saying something completely unexpected.

"I could show you, if you want."

"Show me . . . ?" Jacob looked confused.

"How to bend the bone between your elbow and your wrist," I said.

He didn't answer for a long moment.

"I promise, it's much easier than breathing through your eyelids."

A perplexed smile slowly bloomed on his face.

"But I warn you," I added, "it *is* harder than reading with the soles of your feet."

He didn't laugh. Instead he looked at me curiously.

"You really want to help me?" he asked. "With fiddle?"

I shrugged, then nodded. "Sure."

"But I thought this was your month to get away from all that," Jacob said.

He looked pointedly at my right hand. Not the one with the calluses that he so weirdly thought were awesome. But the one I'd injured in the blacksmithing barn.

"It was," I said haltingly. "I mean, it is. I mean . . . whatever! It'll only take a few minutes."

Jacob paused for a long moment. He seemed to be searching my face.

I'm sure he didn't find anything clarifying there. I myself still wasn't sure why I'd made the offer. Now that I had, I didn't know if I believed what I'd said, that teaching Jacob that fiddle trick was no big deal.

In fact, maybe I'd just done something momentous.

"I'll take those minutes," Jacob said. "How about tomorrow after class? Do you know that little river at the end of the Sap Hill trail?"

Just as I nodded, the Hobart beeped shrilly.

I quickly turned my back to Jacob and hauled the door open, happy to hide my half-giddy, half-panicked face in the resulting billow of steam.

Over on his side, Jacob got back to work too. For the rest of our shift, we didn't talk much. But we did seem to get in sync as we stacked, sprayed, washed, and unloaded the supper dishes. By the end of the evening, we'd reached a rhythm you could almost call musical.

Chapter ● Nine

Ten minutes before class ended in the barn on Friday, most of the guys were putting away their tools. But I was still pounding away, determined to finally get somewhere after an entire week of blacksmithing fails.

Maybe I was also obsessing about my ironwork so I *wouldn't* fixate on the fiddle lesson I'd promised Jacob.

The fiddle lesson that wouldn't come until the end of a very long day in the barn.

The lesson for which I'd carefully straightened my hair and planned an outfit meant to look entirely unplanned (yet still adorable).

I still didn't know exactly *why* I wanted to look adorable. It wasn't like there was anything remotely romantic about teaching someone how to bend the bones in his forearm. Washing 150 sets of dishes seemed equally uninspiring.

And yet . . .

There was something about washing dishes with *Jacob* that threatened to turn me into a puddle of yearning. It could make the next three weeks at Camden that much more torturous.

Or, said a voice in the back of my head, *the next three weeks at Camden could be magical.*

But that seemed unlikely. What hope did I have if even *Annabelle* couldn't make the stars align for herself and Owen? When we'd gone to bed the night before, she'd admitted that she still hadn't talked to him, despite my little pep talk in the dining hall.

"There was just something about the post-dinner vibe that wasn't right," she'd told me as we'd lain side by side in our twin beds. "You have to listen to what the universe tells you. . . . There's a saying from the *I Ching* that goes like this . . . soul mates . . . destiny."

I drifted to sleep while Annabelle went on and on. I didn't need to listen to understand what she was saying: liking a boy was agony. It required superhuman powers of self-distraction.

Thus, my immersion in my ironwork.

Over the course of my day in the barn, I'd finally found a rhythm to my smithery. I pulled my chunk of iron from the forge, then hammered it so hard I felt the jangle travel up my arm and rattle my shoulder in its socket.

Next, I dunked my lump into the water bucket. *Sssssss.*

Then I examined it and noted the infinitesimal changes I'd made with my pathetic Olive Oyl arms.

Then I did it all over again. And again. And again.

Except a funny thing happened the final time I squinted at my metal chunk. It didn't look so chunky anymore. My side-stroking blows had elongated it. My regular turns had shaped the resulting stem into a not-terribly-lopsided cylinder that culminated in a point.

At its other end was a cap that *was* pretty lopsided, but was also unmistakably flat and round.

"Coach! Come here!" I called. I had to restrain myself from squealing in excitement. Blacksmiths swear. They never squeal.

Coach walked over, smoothly and deliberately as he always did. But when he saw what I was holding, clamped in a pair of soot-stained tongs, his sweaty, dirty face lit up.

"Nell! Spike!" he said.

This wasn't some form of football lingo. He was referring to the thing I had made—a six-inch-long, three-pound, crusty-skinned iron spike, perfect for hammering down, say, a railroad tie. I mean, if this were the 1800s and my last name was Lewis or Clark. For my current life and times, the spike was pretty much useless, but at that moment, it was my most prized possession.

"I can't believe I made that!" I said, admiring the brushy hammer strokes visible in the metal.

"I knew you had it in you," Coach said. "You beat the beast."

That was his affectionate name for our massive, belching forge.

"And even," he added slyly, "with a burned hand."

I gulped and clamped my left hand over the fresh scar on my right one.

"You knew about that?" I squeaked.

"Nellie, I see everything," Coach said. Normally, I hated when anyone called me Nellie, but when Coach said it in that dad-like rumble of his, it actually made me happy. So did the respect I saw in his eyes for the first time ever. (At least I thought I saw it. Coach's eyebrows were as bushy and grizzly as his beard, which made his eyes kind of hard to see.)

Mrs. Teagle thought hiding my anvil burn was the height of foolishness. I now realized that Coach might think otherwise. The code of the barn was all about being careful and methodical, making sure you did everything possible to avoid melting your face off. We had a saying that we called out like a battle cry whenever the forge ran too hot or too cold: *Respect the beast!*

If you didn't respect the beast, the iron that you'd been carefully molding for hours could turn into a puddle. Or it wouldn't get molten enough and your next hammer stroke would land so hard, it would make your brain jangle.

But another rule of blacksmithing was this: no whining. It was bad form to grumble about scrapped work, sore muscles, or minor burns. For all I knew, *all* the guys were nursing blistered wounds—and they were as closemouthed about them as I was.

Maybe I wasn't so badly suited for blacksmithing after all.

I carried my spike over to the beat-up wooden table where we were supposed to leave our finished work. I scanned the other smiths' pieces—several really respectable horseshoes, a twisty fireplace poker, and some surprisingly delicate candlesticks. All these items were much more polished than my lowly spike, but I didn't care. My nubbly nail reminded me of the scruffiest puppy in a litter, the one you chose out of pity, then adored more fiercely than any perfect, pedigreed dog.

I put my spike on the table, gave it a little pat, then turned to head out. But Coach stopped me.

"You should take it with you," he said, nodding at my spike. "It's your first one. There's nothing like it."

I blushed, then laughed to cover up the blush.

"What am I gonna do, put it under my pillow?" I joked. "Or hang a really, really big picture on the wall?"

"Just hold it in your hand," Coach said, not joining in on my laughter or even smiling. To him, even my overgrown thumbtack was a sacred thing.

"Just take in all those beautiful flaws," Coach went on, "all those dents and scars that say, 'A person made this. *I* made this.'"

Who knew Coach, who routinely spat on the floor, could be so poetic? I think he was almost more moved by my success than I was.

But I did take him up on his offer and carried my spike, cradled in both hands, out of the barn.

It was only then that I realized I'd been too successful at distracting people that day. While pounding out my ridiculously large nail, I'd truly forgotten about the fiddle lesson with Jacob.

And now, I was late.

There was no time to go back to my dorm and shower. No time to restraighten my hair or put on that perfectly imperfect outfit.

I rolled my eyes, shoved my spike into the back pocket of my cut-offs, and used the barnyard pump to splash some water on my face.

Oh well, I sighed as I hurried away from the barn. *I guess that's another way to avoid obsessing about a boy—show up at your romantic meeting place looking sooty, sweaty, and frizzy-haired. If there was a spark there, it's going to go out as soon as he lays eyes on me.*

Chapter ☙ Ten

I felt short of breath as I hurried up the steepest but quickest trail on Sap Hill. The pine sap that gave this hill its name smelled uncomfortably sharp. My nose and throat were already a little dry and raw after my day hovering over the forge.

But the trail through the endless skinny pine trunks was so peaceful and pretty that I couldn't help but calm down.

Maybe this is for the best, I thought, noting that my cuticles were ragged and black, rounding out my grimy appearance just perfectly. *If Jacob finds me not at all attractive, it takes the pressure off. I can be around him without feeling like a swoony spaz. I can breathe.*

With every step through the woods, I felt more certain about this conclusion. More calm. More remote.

Endless iced coffees and ice cream cones with my friends,

bouncing from the city pool to impromptu backyard parties, then back to the pool. Clothes shopping in all my favorite thrift stores. Being allowed to spend entire days in the hammock because I'd be working my way through my school summer reading list.

I got so absorbed in my back-home reverie that I stopped seeing the golden sunlight beaming through the pines. I no longer heard the eerie echoes of birds and bugs, or the burble of the creek up ahead of me. I was lost in the rhythmic *crunch, crunch, crunch* of my boots on the pine needle path until—

> *"I worked in a cotton mill all of my life*
> *Ain't got nothing but this barlow knife*
> *It's hard times, Cotton Mill Girls,*
> *It's hard times everywhere."*

That was Jacob's voice. Jacob's voice *singing* one of Nanny's favorite songs.

I stopped in my tracks, just a few feet from the point where the trail and trees ended, opening up onto the sandy, sun-drenched riverbank.

Jacob was done singing now and was playing the same stanza on the fiddle. This was another technique I recognized from Nanny's class. She always made her students sing their songs before learning them, then continue "singing" in their heads as they played.

He sang again.

"Us kids worked fourteen hours a day
For thirteen cents of measly pay
It's hard times, Cotton Mill Girls,
It's hard times everywhere."

My breath quickened. Hearing Jacob sing about being a put-upon mill worker should have been funny, right? Pathetically adorable, maybe. It definitely shouldn't have been hot.

But oh, it was.

I fisted my fingers and scrubbed my nails on my cutoffs, trying to buff the black off my cuticles. Then I smoothed and smoothed my hair back with sweaty palms before taking a gulp of piney air and stepping out of the trees.

"Sorry I'm late," I called. It was supposed to come out all cheerful and breezy. It was supposed to say, *Of* course *I didn't just hear you singing "Cotton Mill Girls."*

Instead it sounded more like a nervous bark.

Jacob had been facing the river. When he heard my voice, he spun around to look at me and . . . well, his face lit up.

Like he'd been waiting all day to lay eyes on me.

Part of me wanted to hover at the end of the riverbank, shadowed by the trees and far enough away from Jacob that he wouldn't be able to see what I looked like (and maybe smelled like) up close.

I didn't count on him coming over to me.

"I was worried you weren't coming," he said. "You know, what with your fiddle aversion and all. Speaking of, where is your fiddle?"

"Oh!" I said. "I was going to go back to my room and get rea—and get it. But I got waylaid in the barn, so I just came straight here."

"Oh," he said, nodding slowly.

"But I don't really need to play to explain the whole bendy bone thing to you," I continued nervously. "It's really all a mind trick, since, you know, you can't *really* bend that bone."

"Finally, the truth comes out!" Jacob said to the sky, pumping his bow in the air. Then he looked at me with a smile. "Your grandma totally won't admit that your forearm is not really bendable."

"Nanny has a very active imagination," I said with a giggle. "Promise you won't tell her the truth about the Easter Bunny."

He laughed and gazed at me.

And I gazed back, momentarily forgetting about how gross I looked. Momentarily forgetting what we were even doing there until—

"Okay," Jacob breathed. He took a step closer to me and seemed to lean down. He brought his face close enough to mine that I could see the tired shadows beneath his eyes. "Ready?"

My eyes widened. *Ready for what? Is he going to kiss me?*

Still gazing at me, Jacob lifted his violin and began playing.

Oh, right, I thought drily. *Ready for that.*

Gritting my teeth with the effort, I dragged my eyes from Jacob's face to his bowing arm. Even though his notes did sound clear and sweet, I could tell that something was off in his movements. There was a stiffness there. A lack of bounce.

"I think it's your wrist," I said. "Definitely your wrist. You have to loosen it. Make it *just* this side of limp, but in a strong way. Does that make sense?"

"No," Jacob said, giving me a mock glare. "It doesn't."

"Just try it," I urged him.

He played a couple of not-quite-right phrases, and then we frowned at each other.

"Not the wrist?" he said.

"I think you need to bring your elbow into it," I said with a definitive nod. "Probably your shoulder, too. They all have to work together, but also independently. Does *that* make sense?"

"Nell," Jacob said seriously.

"Yeah?" I bit my lip. I was clearly making a mess of this.

"You know you're not getting out of this without just *showing* me, don't you?"

Jacob held out his violin to me.

I stared at it, hesitant. A few months earlier, my oldest cousin, Lucy, had had a baby girl, and I'd gone to visit her. She'd held her firstborn out to me to hold. I'd been terrified that I'd squeeze too hard or drop her or otherwise do wrong by this tiny, fragile thing who was now the center of Lucy's world.

That's just about how it felt taking Jacob's fiddle.

I lifted it slowly to my shoulder. The chin rest was warm and so was the fiddle's neck. I let my eyes fall closed, and I started to play the same tune Jacob had.

At first I focused on making my arm do all the things I'd just described.

But only a couple of phrases in, my mind wandered. It's what always happened to me when I played something so familiar. I forgot myself. My technique went out the window, along with my counting. I even lost awareness of the fiddle. I simply made music.

When this happened at home, I'd usually emerge from my musical trance to find Nanny waiting for me on the other end, ready with a list of all the things I'd done wrong.

When the song ended and I opened my eyes, Jacob's mouth was hanging open.

"Oh my God, I'm sorry," I said. "I forgot to focus on the bowing arm thing. I always do that."

"Don't apologize!" Jacob said. "That was . . . amazing. I mean, at first you looked kind of stiff and gimpy, frankly."

"Thanks a lot." I laughed. "I can tell you've been learning from Nanny."

"But then . . . ," Jacob said, "you just, it was like the music was controlling you instead of the other way around. How did you *do* that?"

I shrugged.

"I thought I knew," I said. "I really thought I could tell you. But . . . I guess it just *happens*."

"Yeah, if your last name is Finlayson and you've been playing since you were *born*."

Jacob looked crestfallen, and I had to fight the urge to thrust his fiddle back into his arms and run away. But he was right. It wasn't fair that I could do this stupid bendy arm thing that I didn't give a hoot about—and he couldn't.

On the other hand, that gave me an idea.

"Jacob, tell me what you're thinking about when you play this song," I said.

"Well, I'm thinking about the words to the song," he said, ticking it off on his finger. "You know, like your grandma says. And I'm remembering to keep my left wrist dropped and those fingers curved. And on my bowing arm, it's all about trying to relax and loosen up."

"Which is hard to do when you *think* about it," I said, handing him the fiddle. "Play the song really fast and really sloppy."

"Why?" he blurted.

"To see if it's in your bones," I said.

He squinted at me like I'd just spoken a foreign language, but then he did it. His playing was squawky and offbeat, but every note *was* just right.

"All right," I said when he'd finished. "Now I want you to play without thinking about any of that technique stuff you just told me."

"But isn't working on my technique the whole point?"

"Up *to* a point," I said. "But then I think you should just forget about it and *play*."

He frowned at me.

I shrugged.

"Listen, there's a very good chance that it's a *good* thing I'm not Nanny's teaching assistant," I said. "I've never exactly been a rule follower when it comes to music."

"Or when it comes to burglarizing infirmaries," Jacob added.

But as he said it, he smiled.

And then he started playing.

And just like I'd been, he was stiff and stilted at first. I could tell he couldn't bring himself to turn off his brain.

Before I could think twice about it, I jumped behind him and grabbed his shoulders.

"Don't stop!" I said when his bow squawked and threatened to come to a halt. I prodded him until he'd turned to face the river, where a mini rapid of white foam was swooshing around a series of rocks.

"There's rhythm and beauty and any other inspiration you could want right there," I said over the sound of his playing. "Look at that."

He did, and a moment later, I watched his arm go rubbery, as fluid as the water he was looking at.

"You did it!" I squealed. "You bent your forearm!"

Jacob paused in his playing and stared at me.

"I did not!"

"You did!" I insisted. "I saw it with my own eyes."

He stared at the fiddle and bow in his hands and looked around wildly. And all of a sudden, I knew.

He wanted to find a place to toss those things so he could

throw his arms around me. Maybe even pick me up and swoop me around. Maybe even kiss me.

And it might have been amazing.

But it would also have ripped him out of that moment, that pure instance of the Joy that I knew Jacob had been looking for all week, maybe all his life.

I couldn't bear to let him step away from it for even a moment. Even for me.

So I cried out, "Don't stop. You're in it! Keep going!"

With an exuberant laugh, he started playing again.

And again, he nailed that indescribable, rubbery-limbed sweet spot where he'd ceased to play an instrument and started making *music*.

He was so full of the Joy that for a moment, I actually wished I had my fiddle with me so I could join in.

But then I spotted a nicely graspable stone just at the edge of the river and remembered what I had in my back pocket.

An instant later, I was backing Jacob up with a little percussion—tapping that rock against my iron spike with sweet little clangs. I sang, too.

> *"When I die don't bury me at all*
>
> *Just hang me up on the spinning room wall*
>
> *Pickle my bones in alcohol,*
>
> *It's hard times everywhere."*

Just as when we'd sung "Clementine" together, I barely noticed the dreariness of the lyrics. As the last note rang out, then drifted away into the sky and the woods, Jacob whooped with joy.

"Yeah!" he yelled. "I can't believe we did that. And with you playing a . . . a nail?"

I laughed and shrugged.

"Spoons, washboards, nails, whatevs," I said. "Hey, do you like it? I made it!"

I held out my spike for him to see.

"It's . . ." He smiled politely, at a loss for words.

"It's okay," I said with a laugh. "It's a big-ass, bizarro nail, but I'm still in love with it. Because it used to be just a chunk of metal. I hammered it into submission!"

"That's great," Jacob said.

But his smile had faded, and he no longer sounded poised to scoop me into a celebratory hug. I dropped my hand and resisted the urge to hide the spike behind my back like a little kid.

"You think it's dumb," I said.

"No!" Jacob protested. "But—"

He halted, but I gave him a look that said, *You can't get out of this now. Just come out and say it.*

"It just kind of kills me that you can do *this*," Jacob said, holding up his fiddle and bow, "like, *so* much better than me. But you choose to do . . ."

His eyes fell on my spike.

". . . that."

I felt heat rush to my face.

"So you don't think I should have a choice in the matter?" I said. "I should just join the family business whether I want to or not?"

"No," Jacob said quietly. "I just don't believe that you really don't want that. Not when you play fiddle the way you do. Not when you can't help but turn a railroad spike into an instrument."

I blinked at Jacob.

And that's when I realized that there were two sides to swooning.

A moment ago Jacob had looked past the black circles ringing my nails, my ash-dusted skin, and my dirty tank top. He'd seemed to swoon for me.

But maybe the swoon had only happened because Jacob had thought that I was just like him. He couldn't understand that music was an obligation for me, a tether holding me back. All he knew was what it was for *him:* a pair of wings, setting him free.

He didn't really see me. He saw who he wanted to see, and *that's* who he liked.

I couldn't speak.

Because when your heart hurts as badly as mine did, it takes your breath away.

That makes it hard to dash into the woods and hurry back to your dorm, then linger too long in a shower and maybe even cry a little bit.

But those things—I managed to do.

Chapter ● Eleven

After my shower, I didn't have the heart to do my usual twenty-minute hair ritual, slathering it with product, then laboriously blowing it straight. Instead I just flopped onto my bed, grabbed my e-reader, and spent the twenty minutes staring at it without comprehending a word.

Annabelle came back to our room just before dinner. She froze in the doorway and said, "Oh! Your hair!"

I jumped, and my hand flew to my now-dry hair. It felt soft and poufy—like a dandelion.

"Uh-oh, how bad is it?" I said, swinging myself off the bed. "I got it cut into this bob a few weeks ago, and I haven't let it air-dry since."

When I peeked into the mirror over the dresser, I gasped.

"I look like a goth Orphan Annie!" I whisper-screamed. My hair had frizzed into ringlets that sproinged up and out all over my head. So not only did it feel like a dandelion, with its fuzzy, spherical shape, it looked like one too.

"Urgh," I groaned. "By the time I get this straightened out, I'm going to completely miss dinner."

Annabelle frowned at me.

"Nell, can I give you some advice?"

Normally, I would have hesitated. Every time Annabelle offered me advice, she used all these life-coachy terms like "listen to the universe" and "get in touch with yourself." All of it made zero sense to me.

My mom, on the other hand, would have loved Annabelle. They both did yoga and wore the kind of gauzy skirts you can buy off a street rack for fifteen dollars apiece.

Also like Annabelle, my mom wore her curls long. They trailed down her back, all soft and springy, the same dark-blond color my hair had been before I dyed it. Black and blunt suited me better, or so I'd thought.

But given my currently desperate situation, I said to Annabelle, "Okay, yes. Please tell me what to do about this mess."

"Well, don't call it a mess, for starters," Annabelle said. "Your hair is part of you. You have to embrace it. You have to love it!"

"Easy for you to say," I said, pointing at her glossy, tightly corkscrewed mane. It was tied loosely at the nape of her neck, and a few tendrils bounced adorably on her cheeks. "You've got the hair of a goddess."

"Well, it's *not* easy," she reprimanded. "I *hope* I don't have to tell you about the history of African-American women and their hair."

I tried not to sigh as Annabelle launched into a lecture about the social politics of hot combs and relaxers. I wondered if she ever got tired of being so *meaningful*.

As she moved onto a history lesson about Madam C. J. Walker, she also began to work on my hair. She sprayed it down with a water bottle, then worked some fruity-smelling hair gel through it. She quickly worked her way around my head, coiling small sections of my hair around her fingers. Finally she grabbed a couple of lobster-claw clips out of a dish on her dresser and loosely clipped my bangs back at the temples.

"And . . . done," Annabelle said. She put her hands on my shoulders and turned me toward the mirror.

My mouth popped open.

My hair was frizz free. The curls that had been standing straight up, looking frazzled and angry, were now prettily framing my face. But I hadn't been transformed into a clone of Annabelle or my mom. My hair was still a bit blunt and edgy, the way I liked it, but instead of being crisp and straight-edged, it looked light and springy.

It had taken Annabelle all of five minutes to achieve.

"You're welcome," Annabelle said, before I could get it together to thank her.

"I—I love it!" I said.

"Just promise me you'll *own* it," Annabelle said. "Your hair is *you*, Nell. Always remember that."

I nodded even as I was thinking, *No, Annabelle. Hair is just hair.*

Nevertheless, I did feel kind of different, even floaty, as Annabelle and I walked together to the dining hall. Something about my head feeling so light and breezy made my hurt feelings lighten too.

That didn't mean I was ready to face Jacob yet. At our table, I strategically positioned myself three seats away from him. I was far enough from him that we couldn't talk, yet close enough that we couldn't make eye contact across the table. Our view of each other was blocked by Marnie and Isabelle chatting animatedly between crunchy bites of radish salad.

I ate as quickly as possible and headed for the kitchen. Not only did I have Jacob to avoid, it was fried chicken night again, and I really didn't need to watch all the carnivores enjoying their dinners, not tonight, when I really could have used some comfort food.

There is *nothing* comforting about radish salad.

In the kitchen, I gave the staffers a quick, morose wave hello, then headed for the supply closet to tie on my apron and grab my hat. When I made to leave the closet, though, Jacob was blocking the door and *looking* at me.

My body seemed to be running a few hours behind, because as usual, my heart quickened and my cheeks went hot at the sight of him.

But my brain. It was weary and sad after the day's emotional roller coaster.

"What is it, Jacob?"

"Your hair . . . ," he said.

"Oh, that." I gave my ringlets a self-conscious pat. "Annabelle did it."

"It's . . ." Jacob stopped himself, then started over. "Well, it looks nice."

Inexplicably, this made a lump form in my throat. So I just stared at the floor and gave him a quick nod of thanks before pushing past him out of the closet.

"Hey," Ms. Betty called from the stainless-steel table where she was cutting butter into a big bowl of flour. "Don't forget your hat, sweetheart."

"Oh yeah," I muttered, glancing down at the baseball cap, forgotten in my hand. I smushed it down over my curls.

I trudged to the dining hall window to load the first wave of dishes onto the cart. Next, I should have delivered them to Jacob, who was waiting at the sink. But I still didn't feel fully ready to face him. So I stopped and called out across the kitchen, "Ms. Betty, the scones at breakfast this morning were delicious."

"They were *not*," Ms. Betty said, waving me off with a plump hand. "They looked terrible."

"Well, yeah, they *were* pretty ugly," I admitted. "But they *tasted* amazing. That's what matters."

"Well, bless your heart," Betty twanged at me. In the next

instant, though, her rosy, smiling face went hard. "But you're all wrong, kid. Martha Stewart's scones are perfect golden triangles, and so shall mine be. You'll see."

"I'm rootin' for you," I said while Ms. Betty laughed.

I laughed too. It calmed me enough to deal with Jacob. I pushed the cart toward him, my head ducked low. The brim of my baseball cap prevented me from meeting his eyes.

But I couldn't help spotting the plate he held in his hands. It wasn't an empty, waiting to be scrubbed. In fact, it was neatly covered with a grease-dotted paper napkin.

"I—I got this for you," Jacob said, thrusting the plate toward me.

Warily, I stepped around the dish cart, took the plate, and peeked beneath the napkin.

Then I nearly swooned.

Jacob had given me a piece of fried chicken.

It was a big drumstick with a deep-brown crust. I could tell, without even touching it, that it was super crunchy, just the way I liked it. It smelled better than delicious—it was intoxicating.

I stared at Jacob.

"But—?"

"Listen, I was an idiot earlier," he said. "I want to apologize."

My knees suddenly felt weak, either from the apology or the smell of the fried chicken. Probably a little of both.

"But," I said, "why are you apologizing with . . . a chicken leg?"

"Nell." Jacob's serious sorry-face was starting to twitch with amusement. "I know."

"You know *what*?"

"I know," he repeated, failing to fight off a smile, "you're not really a vegetarian."

I opened my mouth to protest, but I didn't have the energy. I slumped as I admitted, "You're right. I'm a total carnivore. And I've never been so hungry in my life. Is it that obvious?"

"Only on fried chicken night," Jacob said with a grin.

A clatter at the dining room window made us jump. Two tall stacks of plates had just arrived.

Painfully, I re-covered the chicken leg.

"No, no," Jacob said. "You eat, I'll start the dishes."

"Jacob," I said, "you *know* I'm not going to eat meat in front of you. Not after the whole Sally thing."

"What if I promise to eat something you don't like in front of you?" Jacob bargained.

"Already done," I said. "It doesn't get any grosser than radish salad."

"Hey, I heard that!" Ms. Betty squawked, glaring at me over her sticky scone dough.

Clang!

A bowl full of clattery silverware appeared in the window. Jacob pointed at the screened door that led to a patio behind the dining hall.

"Listen," he said. "I promise you, being a vegetarian is my thing. I honestly don't care what anybody else does. So, go."

I stared down at the plate in my hands.

And I went.

Outside, I sat on a bench looking out at an empty, grassy field. A breeze seemed to amplify the scent of the fried chicken, making it officially irresistible.

I took a bite.

It was so delicious, I had to suppress a groan. With each successive mouthful, I felt happier—and not just because I felt truly full for the first time all week.

When I returned to the kitchen, the Hobart was beeping insistently. I whipped the tray out and began cheerfully stacking hot, clean dishes.

"Thank you," I said to Jacob on the other side of the Hobart. "And thanks for being non-judgey about the whole carnivore thing."

"I'm really not," Jacob assured me, nodding his head emphatically. "But I am kind of curious . . ."

"About why I'm a completely fraudulent vegetarian?" I said. "At the time, I didn't really think about what I was doing. I guess I just wanted to do something, anything, unexpected. And not just surprising to Nanny or the rest of my family, but to *me*. So I became a vegetarian blacksmith. I guess I didn't completely think it through, though. That this would be my *life* for the next thirty days."

"So how does it feel now?" Jacob asked.

"It feels . . . well, surprising, for sure!" I said with a laugh. "I barely recognize myself, especially now."

I flicked at one of my curls with a fingertip.

Of course, I didn't tell him the biggest surprise of all—how I felt about him. He made me both swoony and wary, ambivalent and obsessed. I barely knew him, and yet half the time, I could have sworn I knew what he was thinking.

Of course, the other half, I had *no* idea what he was thinking. Particularly, what he was thinking about *me*.

Part of me wanted to retreat into the blacksmithing barn, where the only hurts I risked were burns and bruises.

But the other part of me—most of me—was dying to see what would happen next between me and Jacob.

Chapter ● Twelve

To say I was nervous the next night—our last night in the kitchen—would be an understatement. Twenty-four hours after the Drumstick, I still didn't know how to feel.

Was I relieved that our punishment was almost over? And that somehow over the past two nights, I'd managed to evade Nanny's detection? (It helped that teachers never cleared dishes, an honor strictly enforced at Camden.)

Or was I bereft about saying good-bye to these evenings with Jacob?

As he and I walked together from the dining hall to the kitchen door, we were both quiet. Too quiet.

So, of course, I had to go fill the awkward silence with even more awkward small talk.

"So . . . have you had a nightmare about Hobart yet? Heh, heh."

I turned my head so he wouldn't see me roll my eyes at my own lameness.

But Jacob just shook his head.

"Hobart's not so bad," he said. "As long as you respect the beast, right?"

I looked at him in surprise.

"That's so funny, that's what we say in blacksmithing," I said. "About the forge."

Now Jacob looked a little squirmy.

"Oh, um, yeah, I knew that," he said. "I ran into Clint earlier. We were talking about blacksmithing . . . and stuff."

"Oh," I said, pushing open the kitchen door. "What kind of stu—"

Before I could say anything else, Ms. Betty's voice rang out, practically making my eyeballs rattle.

"That's it!" she cried. "#$&%ing Martha Stewart!"

"Whoa," I whispered to Jacob. "That's something *else* we say in blacksmithing. Minus the Martha Stewart part."

While Jacob laughed, I headed for Ms. Betty.

"What happened?"

But as soon as I reached her, the answer was evident. She was staring at a half-sheet pan that she'd clearly tossed onto the worktable. It was covered with three-cornered lumps, walnut brown and puckered. They resembled the gravel in the parking lot more than baked goods.

"Fig balsamic scones," Ms. Betty said with a curled lip.

"Oh," I said. "Well, maybe you could tr—"

"I'm making cinnamon rolls instead, durn it!" Ms. Betty screeched. As she began slamming around measuring cups, I retreated to the dishwasher.

"Hobart seems absolutely tame," I whispered to Jacob, "now that I've experienced the wrath of Ms. Betty."

He laughed again as he shoved the first tray of dishes into the churning washer.

"Don't let Hobart hear you say that," he said. "You don't want him to get revenge."

I giggled as we settled into the now-comfortable rhythm of ferrying dishes to and fro, of spraying and stacking and pulling and unloading.

Behind us, Ms. Betty seemed to take about three minutes to whip up her cinnamon roll dough. As she began to knead, she turned up the radio, which was tuned to an oldies station.

A moment later, though? "Respect" came on—and Ms. Betty started dancing.

Now, Ms. Betty was not a small woman. In fact, she was probably about the same size as Aretha Franklin, who was singing the song. So even though Ms. Betty didn't jump while she danced, all her body parts *did*.

"Ooh, I'm jiggling like a jelly doughnut over here," she whooped.

My effort to suppress a laugh was desperate and futile. The

laugh happened and it happened big, accompanied by a tremendous snort.

Then Jacob started laughing. I don't know if it was my snort that got to him or Ms. Betty's bounce.

Luckily, Ms. Betty laughed along with us.

"Oh, I know I should lose a few pounds, she admitted. "Okay, fifty. But I'm so much happier when I can *eat*."

"Amen, Ms. Betty!" I said, holding my wet, soapy hand out for a high five.

Instead she grabbed my hand and pulled me away from the sink. She propelled me into a spin, and before I knew it, we were bumping hips and whooping it up.

"Shake what you got, girl, even if you don't got much!" Ms. Betty hollered.

I would have blushed at her comment about my non-figure, but I was having too much fun. So I just rolled my eyes at Ms. Betty and kept dancing, doing a simultaneous heel spin and head bobble.

By the time I finished my twirl, Ms. Betty had yanked *Jacob* away from the dishes. Then, with our hands still in hers, she turned us toward each other and sashayed backward, extricating herself from our little dance party.

For a moment, we froze. Jacob looked a little panicked, and I'm sure I did too.

"Dance," Ms. Betty ordered us.

We danced.

At first we did it with irony, exchanging a silent we're-just humoring-our-elder-and-nobody-shall-know-of-this promise.

But then Aretha started chanting, "*R-E-S-P-E-C-T, find out what it means to me. R-E-S-P-EEEE-C-T . . .*"

And, well, I defy anyone not to go wild when you get to that part of the song.

I threw my arms over my head and swiveled like a corkscrew. Jacob started pogoing.

A moment later we were singing along: "*Sock it to me, sock it to me, sock it to me, sock it to me!*" and dancing together. We quickly found a rhythm. When I swayed backward, he swayed forward, and vice versa. Our faces moved so close together that I could see tiny beads of sweat on Jacob's upper lip and I could smell the sharp, clean scent of his skin.

That's when I stopped singing. I couldn't inhale Jacob's wonderful smell and shout "*Sock it to me*" at the same time.

But I didn't stop dancing, not until the last note thrummed out of the radio. When it did, Jacob and I landed with thuds, breathing hard, our cheeks flushed. I giggled while Jacob swiped at his forehead with his T-shirt sleeve.

Only then did we realize that Ms. Betty had disappeared into the big walk-in pantry on the other side of the kitchen.

We were alone.

And our faces were still very, very close together.

This was the moment when we should have pulled away from each other, laughing and rolling our eyes at our own goofiness.

But the moment passed and we didn't move. We remained eye to eye.

I couldn't catch my breath, and it wasn't from the singing and dancing.

Just when I felt my lips tingle in anticipation, just when my eyelids began to flutter closed, just when I thought that something momentous was about to happen between Jacob's mouth and mine, the kitchen door slammed open.

Jacob and I jumped apart. Then we spun around to find Mrs. Teagle standing in the doorway, one shocked hand on her mama-bird chest. She looked from us to the floor beneath our feet to our dishwashing station.

I looked around too, noticing for the first time the chaos that our little dance party had wrought. There were puddles of soapy water on the floor and a pile of unrinsed dishes congealing in the sink. The Hobart's green light indicated that a tray of dishes was long finished and waiting to be unloaded. I guess I hadn't heard the beep over the loud music.

"My lord!" Ms. Teagle said, turning the radio off. "What's been going on here? You can hear the noise almost up to the great hall!"

"Oh, Mrs. Teagle," I gasped. "Um . . . what's going on is . . ."

I looked pleadingly at Jacob for help.

"We were moved by the music, ma'am," Jacob said seriously. "We started dancing. *You* can understand, can't you? I mean, as director of a school that's all about music and art?"

I had to bite my lip hard to keep from laughing.

"I understand that you don't seem to be taking your punishment very seriously," Mrs. Teagle said with a frown. "I'm of a mind to give you kids another night of dish duty to teach you a lesson about finishing what you've started."

I gave Jacob a quick glance, looking for the telltale neck splotches he got when he was upset.

They weren't there.

But when I looked at his eyes to see what other emotional intel I could glean, his glasses were too soap-speckled and steam-fogged to see anything.

As we waited for Mrs. Teagle to pronounce our fate, I felt something like hope. It seemed I *did* want to spend another night with pruney fingers, scalded skin, hat-head . . . and Jacob.

But Mrs. Teagle shrugged.

"Just get the dishes finished and clean up the rest of this mess," she said with a tight smile, "and we'll call it even. I think it's time for everyone to get back to their normal schedules anyway."

She peered around the kitchen, and only when it was clear that Ms. Betty wasn't within earshot, added, "I've gotten a few complaints about the scones. They're too fancy! It's time for Ms. Betty to give up on that Yankee."

"You mean Martha Stewart?" I squeaked. "*That* Yankee?" Having to hold in so much laughter was making my stomach muscles hurt!

"No worries, Mrs. Teagle," Jacob said. He pointed at the

baking counter, where a couple of deep steel pans held Ms. Betty's expanding yeast dough. "Those are going to be cinnamon rolls in the morning."

"Mmm, Betty's cinnamon rolls," Mrs. Teagle purred, a dreamy smile on her face. "Now that's more like it."

She looked at her watch.

"Shame you'll miss the sing-along tonight," she said. "It's over in twenty minutes. But I would like to see you there tomorrow."

She glared at us, and her voice went sharp again.

"Am I clear?" she said.

"Yes, ma'am," Jacob and I said automatically.

"All righty, then," Mrs. Teagle burbled. Like so many Southern ladies, she was an expert at turning charm into menace and back again. "Good night, darlings."

After Mrs. Teagle left, Jacob and I allowed ourselves one more belly laugh before we got back to work.

We'd become such experts at loading and unloading the Hobart that we didn't even finish much later than usual. After we'd transferred the last stack of dishes to a clean cart, we used rags to soak up the puddles on the floors.

Jacob scoured the sink with what seemed like extra attention, and I used stainless-steel cleaner on the counters instead of the usual spray bottle of soapy water. I buffed them until they shone.

After that, we looked at each other blankly. There was nothing left to do.

Together we looked over at Ms. Betty. She was back at

her work, hauling out baking pans, a rolling pin, and other pastry-making tools.

Jacob looked at me and raised his eyebrows in a question.

I knew exactly what he was asking. I didn't think twice about my answer.

"Ms. Betty," I called across the kitchen, "want some help with those?"

She laughed.

"What? Haven't you had enough of this place yet?"

"We're just angling for a hot cinnamon bun," Jacob said.

"Well, too bad for you, these are rising overnight and won't be ready till tomorrow," Ms. Betty said.

Jacob shrugged and grinned.

"Oh well," he said. "Then I guess we'll be on our way—"

"Hold it right there!" Ms. Betty cried, pointing at us with her rolling pin. "You offered. I'm acceptin'. Get some clean aprons on and get yourselves over here."

We spent the next forty-five minutes rolling out spongy swaths of dough, sprinkling them with a streusel of butter, sugar, and cinnamon, and coiling it all into spirals. Ms. Betty then used a scary-looking cleaver to chop the long rolls into fist-size buns.

As we worked, we sang along with more Motown songs, told jokes, and snuck tastes of the streusel.

Then, when there was *really* nothing left to do, Jacob and I hugged Ms. Betty good-bye and left the kitchen. By then, my fingers had unwrinkled, and they smelled like cinnamon.

Jacob and I walked slowly toward the dorms. Our feet crunched, crunched, crunched on the gravel path while the crickets and cicadas called to one another. The silence between us was comfortable, until we got to the three-pronged fork in the path. One fork led to the women's and family dorms, one to the men's, and the last headed to the little cottages where Nanny and the other instructors stayed.

The space behind my sternum felt hollow. I somehow recognized the feeling as pre-loneliness.

After tonight, I realized, I would see Jacob only at meals. Those happened three times a day, but they were obviously far from private. They were also often dominated by Annabelle's long lectures and Isabelle and Marnie's quilting-bee gossip. (Okay, the gossip was usually pretty good, but still . . .)

I also realized that even before kitchen duty had turned into a dance party, it had been kind of . . . fun. When can you say that about a dishwashing job?

Except . . . I *wasn't* saying any of this to Jacob. I *couldn't*. It would have been too mortifying.

The one thing I absolutely didn't know about Jacob was whether he was also having these confusing, perhaps-more-than-friend-like feelings about me.

I wasn't about to try to find out.

That's his job, I thought to myself as we stood at the forks in the path, not yet saying good-bye. *If anybody's going to say anything, it's got to be him.*

This *wasn't* because he was the boy and I was the girl.

No, it was because he was the earnest, matter-of-fact one and I was the cagey, embarrassment-prone one.

So I waited one beat longer. Would Jacob seize this perfect opportunity, when the night air smelled cool and sweet and a big crescent moon hung above our heads?

Jacob shoved his hands in his pockets and hunched his shoulders up to his ears. He gazed up at the inky, twinkly sky for a moment.

Then finally, *finally*, he said something.

"I don't think I'll ever forget Ms. Betty dancing to Aretha Franklin," he said.

And even though I was disappointed that he was talking about *Ms. Betty* instead of us, I had to laugh.

"Yeah, that was something to see," I replied.

"It was fun," Jacob said. "Tonight."

I wanted to search his face to see if there was some deeper meaning attached to the statement. *And by fun, I mean dancing with you, making pastry together, and oh yeah, almost kissing next to Hobart.*

You know, something like that.

But Jacob was still gazing up at the stars. I couldn't read his face at all. So I just offered a lame reply.

"It was," I agreed. "Fun."

I waited for him to say something else. Or *do* something else, like take my hand or touch my shoulder or put his lips softly on mine—

"Well, good night!" Jacob said, suddenly tearing his gaze from the sky so he could smile at me. He gave a little wave and abruptly turned to tromp down the path to the men's dorms. He headed away so quickly, I barely had a chance to call after him, "Uh, yeah, good night."

I hoped he couldn't hear the wistfulness in my voice.

As I headed down my own path, I suddenly became very tired. My footsteps grew heavy and shuffling. The scuffing of my boots on the pebbles was so loud that I almost didn't hear Jacob call to me.

Luckily, though, I have the Finlayson ears. I stopped and turned toward him.

"Tomorrow's Sunday," he observed.

"Um, yeah?" I said. It felt awkward talking loudly to each other across the ten-foot pie slice of grass that separated our pathways.

"Well, that means we have the day off," Jacob said. "I think I'm going to take a hike."

"Oh," I replied. "Where are you going?"

"I haven't tried the Saturn trail yet," he said. "You know the one that makes a loop up and down the mountain?"

"I remember that from the last time I was here," I said. "It's a pretty hike. Kind of long, though."

"I like long walks," Jacob said.

I hesitated for a moment before I said, "So do I."

Jacob shrugged.

"Well, I'm going right after breakfast," he said, "if you want to come."

It was not a romantic proposal.

It sounded more like an accidental date, like *I'll be there and you'll be there so we'll both be there, but not really, you know, there together.*

But still, it made that hollow feeling inside my ribs go away. So I nodded at Jacob.

"Right after breakfast," I confirmed.

And when I resumed my walk to my dorm, I found that my step had lightened again and I couldn't stop smiling.

Chapter ● Thirteen

The hike might have been wonderful. There was one rub. Late Saturday night the temperature spiked, rolling in with the dark like a damp, oppressive blanket.

Around midnight, Annabelle and I cranked up our ceiling fan and tossed off our quilts, sleeping only under thin top sheets. At three a.m. I could hear her tossing around, flipping her pillow over in a desperate search for a cool spot. It wasn't there. I knew this because I kept doing the exact same thing.

Finally, around five thirty, we gave up, threw on swimsuits, and headed for the lake with towels draped around our necks.

We kicked off our flip-flops and walked on the grass so our feet wouldn't crunch on the gravel paths, waking up anybody who'd managed to sleep in the heat. We didn't speak for the same reason.

When we reached a safe distance from the dorms, I expected Annabelle to start talking, probably about global warming. So I headed her off at the pass.

"It happens almost every summer, just so you know," I said.

Annabelle turned to me, her eyes cloudy with thought.

"What?" she asked.

"The heat," I said, gesturing through the thick air with a limp hand. "It's not necessarily a sign of the environmental apocalypse. It's just part of living in the South."

When Annabelle didn't respond, I added nervously, "You know, in case you weren't prepared, coming from up north."

"Oh, that," Annabelle said absently. She smiled, even as she lifted her mane of ringlets and fanned the back of her neck with her hand. "Oh, this is so much better than a New York heat wave. There, you have cement baking the soles of your feet and taxis blowing hot air up your legs. And the smell! Ugh. At least here, it feels clean and green."

"And hot," I noted with a laugh in my voice.

"And hot," she said. I was *not* used to such brevity from Annabelle. She was clearly distracted, but I wasn't about to ask her why. Not when the heat was making my brain fuzzy and I hadn't had any caffeine yet.

After another minute or so of silence, Annabelle stopped in her tracks and turned to me.

"How do you do it?" she asked.

"How do I do *what*?" I asked. Annabelle was seventeen, gorgeous, self-assured, and (so she thought) knowledgeable about *everything*. What could I possibly be doing better than her?

"How are you staying so together?" Annabelle asked. "I'm a basket case over Owen, but you, you make falling in love look like a breeze!"

"Love?" I squawked, skidding to a stop in the dewy grass. "Owen? *Love?* Annabelle, what are you talking about?"

"Hello?" she replied. "You and Jacob."

I widened my eyes and started to shake my head.

"I'm not sure if anybody else has caught on to you," she said, ignoring me. "Don't worry. It's just, well, I'm your roommate. And I'm *very* intuitive. Except, well, except when it comes to *my* crush. I'm a nervous wreck, Nell! I mean, do I tell him how I feel? Do I *not* tell him, but just *show* him? Do I just wait for him to come to me? That doesn't seem very feminist, but . . . Anyway, how did it happen for you?"

"How did *what* happen?" I said.

"How did you and Jacob become an item?" Annabelle asked.

"An item?" I squawked again. I was beginning to sound as birdlike as Mrs. Teagle. "Where did you get that idea?"

"Please, you disappear with him every night after dinner," Annabelle said. She set off again toward the lake, and I stumbled after her. "And didn't you go to the river with him a couple of days ago?"

"Well, yes, but—"

"That's *totally* romantic," she said. "I mean, you don't spend that much time with someone that you don't *adore*, you know?"

"I—I *don't* know, Annabelle," I blurted. "It's not like that between me and Jacob. At least I *think* it's not. Not on his part, anyway. Oh, who knows, maybe it is! The bottom line is, I don't know because nothing's happened between us."

"Really?" Annabelle asked skeptically.

"I'm pretty sure I'd remember if I'd kissed Jacob," I replied with an eye roll.

"Just because you aren't kissing," Annabelle said, "doesn't mean nothing's happening between you."

"Oh," I said. I blinked as I pictured Jacob's smile, which seemed different, special, when it was directed at me.

Then I thought about our time together and that thing he'd said to me in the kitchen, the compliment lost to the cacophony of the dishwasher.

I remembered him bent over the infirmary doorknob with my bobby pin, taking a risk for me.

As Annabelle and I rounded the thicket of trees that separated the lake from the rest of campus, she said something else.

"A few nights ago, you told me I shouldn't overthink things with Owen," she said. "But maybe *you* should be thinking about things with *Jacob* a little more."

"You know, I think you're ri—"

"Oh my God!" Annabelle cut me off and clutched my arm with the grip of a bird of prey.

"Whoa!" I winced. "Were you always this strong or is it the pottery lessons?"

"He's here!" Annabelle whisper-shrieked. "Owen!"

She motioned with her head at the lake, while also averting her eyes from it.

I looked, then laughed. There were at least a dozen people splashing around in the water, driven from their beds by the heat, just like us.

One of them was Owen, shaking his wet hair out of his eyes like a happy dog.

And another one was Jacob.

An irrational part of me thought that Jacob must know we'd just been talking about him.

And a *rational* part knew I must look terrible. I was sweaty and disheveled. I hadn't even bothered to brush my hair.

It comforted me a little bit to see that Jacob wasn't wearing his glasses in the water. But obviously, his vision wasn't too terrible, because he spotted me anyway, squinting as he waved.

I needn't have worried about my hair. He seemed oblivious to it. That was because (how could I have forgotten?) I was wearing a two-piece swimsuit. It was my favorite, red and polka-dotted with an amply padded top and high-waisted bottoms that made me look like I had hips.

Jacob's eyebrows shot up to his hairline.

"Mm-*hmm*," Annabelle said.

"Shut up!" I whispered, feeling panicky.

"Hi, there!" Annabelle called. There was a flirty lilt to her voice, and it was clear she thought I should adopt the same tone.

But I wasn't a flirty kind of girl in the best of circumstances. My throat was dry and my tongue was completely tied.

This might have been because Jacob was wearing a swimsuit too—long, navy-blue trunks that sat low on his hips so I could see the faint pop of muscles in his abs and the way his shoulders and chest were so much broader than his narrow waist.

After a pause that was way too long on *both* our parts, Jacob said, "Hey, have you guys met Owen? He's in the woodworking class."

I watched as Owen's and Annabelle's eyes met. Her face glowed.

The sight of *her* seemed to knock him so off-balance that he tipped into the water with a splash. But when he came up, he was smiling.

"Come on in," he said to Annabelle (completely ignoring me, which was just fine). "The water's on its way to warm, but it's not there yet."

"You don't have to ask me twice," Annabelle said. The flirt was gone from her voice. And in its place? I heard a note of hope.

She dropped her flip-flops to the sandy dirt and plunged into the water, whooping.

She and Owen quickly commenced chatting. As they drifted into deeper water, I could hear snatches of Annabelle's words.

". . . glaciers melting . . . sustainability . . . Green party . . ."

But instead of looking bewildered or sleepy, the way I often did when Annabelle launched into one of her well-meaning lectures, Owen nodded emphatically.

"Exactly!" he said, pumping his fist so hard that he sprayed Annabelle's face with water. She laughed and splashed him back.

"And they're off," I whispered to myself with a happy giggle.

"Nell, aren't you coming in too?"

I looked at Jacob, who was waving me into the lake.

I'd always hated the shock of dunking myself into cold water. Usually I inched my way in slowly and painfully, immersing my ankles, then knees, then hips. . . .

But with Jacob's eyes on me, I felt self-conscious. So I, too, found myself splashing into the water, then diving beneath the surface.

Unlike my roommate, my plunge into the lake wasn't so much about beginning a conversation as it was an effort to hide.

All I could think about was what Annabelle had said. She was right. *Something* was happening between me and Jacob. And if I wasn't careful, I'd do something crazy like grabbing him and kissing him right then and there.

In my bathing suit.

And in front of all these people, many of whom knew my *grandmother*.

It would be a fiasco.

I remembered the excuses Annabelle had made about Owen—about messages from the universe and the misalignment of the stars.

What would it take for the stars to align for me and Jacob? Was it as simple as the right words, the right time?

I didn't know. But I *was* suddenly feeling grateful for the ridiculously early hour. It meant we had the whole day to find out.

Chapter ● Fourteen

Eventually, hunger drew us out of the lake. I wrapped myself in my towel, but Jacob just let the beads of water stream down his bare chest and shoulders. It was hard not to stare.

"Still want to hike after breakfast?" he asked me.

In this heat?

But what I *said* was, "Sure!"

"Okay," Jacob said. "I'll meet you outside the lodge in, say, forty-five minutes?"

"Uh—"

I wanted to ask Jacob why I wouldn't just be seeing him in the dining hall. But before I could, he grinned at me and darted off.

Again, I was partly relieved. I couldn't bear to walk back to the dorms with him while I was drenched and wrapped in a towel.

It was too intimate, like I'd just stepped out of the shower.

After a quick change and primp, I hurried to the dining hall and . . . Jacob wasn't there.

Neither was Annabelle.

I didn't see Owen, either.

Where *was* everybody?

This could have been a prime opportunity to snag myself some real bacon, instead of the leathery facon at our table. But I was too nervous (and hot) to eat much of anything.

Finally it was time to meet Jacob. As I cleared my barely touched dishes, I tried to decide which scenario made me more nervous—Jacob standing me up, or Jacob arriving at the lodge, right on time.

In the end, he wasn't on time.

He was early.

And he was waiting for me with a bulging backpack slung over his shoulders. He was still wearing his swim trunks, but he'd added a T-shirt, the same cross-country one he'd been wearing on our first day at Camden. In each hand, he held a tall water bottle. They were already covered with condensation from the heat.

"Hi," I said as I approached him, trying to keep the wobble out of my voice. "What's in the bag? *Please* don't tell me it's sheet music."

"Lunch!" Jacob said. "I sweet-talked Ms. Betty into packing us something. Don't worry, I've got a lot of ice packs in here."

"That sounds amazing," I said. "Let me carry some."

"Nah, I got it," Jacob said. "We can compromise by eating early. I skipped breakfast."

"And all I had was a little facon."

"How'd that work out for ya?" Jacob asked, giving me a sly smile as he handed me a water bottle.

"Ugh, no comment," I said. "Out of respect for Sally the pig, I'm not going to say what I *really* wanted for breakfast."

"Well, how do you like pimiento cheese sandwiches?" he asked, tapping his backpack. "And peaches and angel food cake?"

"Oh my God, you had me at pimiento cheese," I sighed. "Have you ever had it?"

We started walking toward the Saturn trail.

"Nope," Jacob said. "I think it's another one of those Southern things that I'm going to love."

"Like 'y'all,'" I teased.

"Among others," Jacob said.

This made me go quiet for a quick, breathless moment until I realized, *Of course he's not talking about* you, *Nell. Get a grip!*

"Let's see, let me think of some of my favorite Northern things," I said. We'd just arrived at the trail. Luckily, it cut through the woods and was completely shaded by trees.

I was also happy that the trail was wide enough for us to continue walking side by side.

I looked up at the treetops as I pondered. "Let's see . . . um."

"Oh, come on," Jacob said, throwing his head back to laugh. "You can't think of even one?"

"Snow!" I blurted. "There. I love snow. Not that I've experienced much of it."

"How great would that be today?" Jacob said. "This shade feels good, though. It's almost *cool* in these woods."

"It's *so* not," I scoffed, taking a swig from my water bottle. "It's like the fire swamp in here."

"At least we don't have to worry about any rodents of unusual size," Jacob said.

I literally put a hand over my heart. He'd gotten my *Princess Bride* reference!

As if he'd read my mind, Jacob said, "Best movie ever."

I grinned at him until something occurred to me.

"Maple syrup!" I exclaimed. "That's another Northern thing I like. And bagels. You can*not* get a good bagel in Atlanta."

"Well, now I know what to do when we're back home," Jacob said. "Forget letters. I'll send bagels."

I knew he was joking. Because, who writes letters anymore?

But the part about staying in touch? By bagel if by nothing else? Was that just banter, or did he really mean it?

"Hey, tell me about life in Connecticut," I said.

"Eh, I live in a suburb," Jacob sighed. "When you're there, you could just as well be in Houston or Toronto or Kansas City."

"Oh, come on," I prodded. "No place is *that* generic. Tell me about the pizza, at least."

"Now, that's true," Jacob said. "Our pizza makes those New York bagels bow down in shame."

"Ugh, thinking about pizza is only making me hotter," I said, fanning myself as we trudged up the path.

"You started it!" Jacob said. He rolled his sweating water bottle over his forehead. "Okay, new subject. What'd you do to get shipped off to Camden?"

I rolled my eyes.

"Oh, that," I said. "Well, I know you know about my family's front-porch jams. . . ."

"Yeah," Jacob said. "They sound pretty amazing."

"I guess they are amazing. . . ."

Given how yearning Jacob looked, I didn't want to admit to him how *very* magical the jams could be at this time of year. The air would smell like honeysuckle and barbecue smoke. There'd be paper lanterns glowing in the magnolia tree in our front yard. A rotating assortment of musicians would play on the porch-turned-stage. They played banjos, fiddles, Irish flutes, pennywhistles, dulcimers, and in the case of my mom, an accordion. We'd toss notes and phrases back and forth among one another, like a bunch of athletes playing an easy game of catch. Between music sets, everyone talked and laughed and ate. The food was always pot-luck. Usually there were earthy-crunchy salads and multigrain rolls right next to pulled pork and collard greens, hummingbird cakes and peach pies.

All these dishes were inevitably delicious. Every joke was funny. Every dance ended with a dip.

"They are amazing," I said again, meaning it. "But—and I

know this sounds obnoxious—if you experience the same kind of amazing every other Sunday from the moment you're born? You know what that becomes? A lot less amazing. So . . . I might have snuck away from one of them with my friend Livvie. And I *might* have forgotten my phone and stayed out past my curfew. It was one of those times when I just *do*, instead of thinking. Kind of like the day I got this crazy idea to break into the Camden infirmary. Did I ever tell you about that?"

"Who would do a nutty thing like that?!" Jacob exclaimed.

I laughed and glanced at my burn. It was baby-smooth and pink, still distinct from the rest of my hand but all healed. The day I burned it, and landed myself and Jacob on kitchen duty, seemed like so long ago, though it had only been six days.

We walked in silence for a moment before Jacob said, "I only *wish* my parents put on boringly amazing house concerts."

"Okay, now that you've made me feel like a total brat," I said.

"No way," Jacob said. "I didn't mean it like that. You're just . . . stuck in an ironic situation, I guess. And so am I."

"Why, what *does* your family do with their weekends?" I asked.

"Basketball. UConn basketball. It's kind of a thing where I'm from. Everybody's obsessed. So, our parties are all about dressing in blue and white and eating chicken wings—"

Jacob mimed throwing chicken bones over his shoulder, which made me laugh out loud.

"—and yelling at the TV. That's it. Oh yeah, and during the commercials, they gripe because their youngest kid plays the *violin* instead of B-ball."

I laughed again.

"That's *tragic*," I agreed. "But at least you run, right?"

I pointed at the CROSS-COUNTRY on his T-shirt.

Jacob looked down at his shirt and said, "It's my brother's. He's a senior, and he's got too many varsity letters, and T-shirts, to count."

I nodded in recognition.

"Just like *my* little brother, Carl, is so into music," I said. "He's learning his sixth instrument right now. Or wait, it might be his seventh, I've lost track. Anyway, each one is more ridiculously old-school than the last."

Jacob laughed before taking another gulp of water.

"Seriously," I insisted. "How many ten-year-olds do you know who can play the Jew's harp and the saw?"

"He sounds like a cool kid," Jacob said.

"Oh, he is," I allowed. "He's very sweet about having a black sheep for a sister."

Jacob turned and touched one of my curls.

"Not as black as you used to be," he said.

I pulled the lock of hair out and squinted at it. He was right. The semipermanent black dye was bleeding away, revealing glints of my natural dark gold. I hadn't even noticed.

But Jacob had.

My knees suddenly felt jiggly, which is inconvenient when you're on a hike. I stopped walking and leaned against a tree, pressing my icy water bottle to my neck.

Jacob stopped too and sighed with relief.

"Ugh," he said. "I didn't want to be the first one to give up. But this heat is ridiculous. Want to turn back?"

I did.

But I also didn't. Not when Jacob had packed us a picnic. Not when we were alone out here, where it was beautiful and peaceful, if sweltering.

But what choice did I have? Continuing to trudge along a trail that felt like the first circle of hell wasn't just unromantic—it was dangerous.

I was just about to say as much when I heard something. I cocked my head and pushed myself off the scratchy tree trunk. I held up my finger to Jacob, motioning for him to follow me. Then, still listening hard, I continued along the trail. It took a sharp curve around a cluster of boulders, then tipped downhill for a stretch.

The sound got louder, and it was unmistakable now—burbling water.

After walking about fifty feet more, I finally saw what I'd heard. There was a shallow, but wide, creek about ten steps from the trail. The water's flow was mostly lazy. Only one section had any rush to it. There, the water skimmed over some slick rocks and landed in a gentle froth. That was enough to insure that the water was clean and cool. It must have been an offshoot of the river on Sap Hill.

"Yessss," Jacob said. "Looks like the perfect place for a picnic to me."

"In the water?" I said.

"Sure, why not? I don't mind if my sandwich gets a little soggy."

"But I changed out of my swimsuit," I said, biting my lip.

"Oh," Jacob said, sounding deflated.

Wiping my damp forehead with the back of my wrist, I lowered myself to the creek bank. I plunged my hand into the water and sucked in my breath.

"It's cold," I told Jacob.

"Oh," he said, sounding even more deflated.

"Aw, why not?" I declared, sitting on my backside so I could untie my shoes.

"You're getting in?" Jacob said. "In your clothes?"

"As hot as it is," I said, "they'll dry before we get to the bottom of the mountain. Or they won't. I don't care!"

I grinned as I got back to my feet. Then, for the second time that day, I jumped into the water.

Of course, creeks are not predictable. The part that I jumped into was only a couple of feet deep. That, you could tell from the edge.

But the creek bottom that I'd thought was grippable sand? It was actually mud. Squishy, unstable, *slippery* mud.

"Whoa!" I shrieked, right before I fell into the water. I came up laughing and sputtering, exhilarated by the sudden cold.

I stood up and wrung out the hem of my tank top, but a moment later, Jacob tumbled into the creek, drenching me all over again.

"Hey!" I squealed, kneeling down to swat a handful of water at him.

"Splash all you want. I'm wearing a swimsuit," Jacob teased.

He scooped handful after handful of water at me.

I shrieked again and fought back. Before long, we were in a full-on water fight, complete with hysterical laughter.

But drained as we were from the heat, we quickly got tired and collapsed. I plunked myself near the edge, the better to reach our picnic. Jacob flopped down next to me. He lifted one of his bare feet and watched the mud drip off it.

"Ew," he said, curling his lip.

"Are you kidding?" I said. "That's clay from the deep South. You could pay good money for someone to smear that stuff on your face at a spa."

"Really?" Jacob looked thoughtful. Then he swiped a dollop of mud out of the creek and rubbed it into his cheek.

"Jacob?" I said, biting my lip to keep in my laughter. "I just made that up. That's pretty much just dirt."

"What?!" Jacob cried while I burst out laughing.

The next thing I knew, he'd smeared a stripe of the clay down *my* cheek.

That's when I stopped laughing.

I couldn't feel his touch through the muck, but I still shivered.

Even though Jacob was wet, disheveled, and mud-caked, he looked more perfect than ever.

He'd stopped laughing too.

He shifted to his knees. It would have been the simplest thing in the world for him to lean toward me and put his mouth on mine. Water droplets trembled on his face, and I wanted to kiss them away.

I wanted this to happen.

I was pretty sure Jacob did too. He tilted his head to the side. He stared at me, and for the first time, I noticed that he'd left his glasses on dry land with his shoes and T-shirt. I could really see his eyes for the first time; could see their deep blue color, their intensity, and behind that, a sweetness, a yearning.

Jacob leaned toward me. I closed my eyes.

"Hahahahaha!"

The laughter came from somewhere nearby—very nearby. It made my eyes snap open. I stifled a gasp, turned awkwardly in the water, and peered back toward the trail.

"You are *so* in trouble for that," a girl's voice said.

"Oh, *really?*" a boy replied before laughing along with her.

Their voices were playful and flirty, and their "fight" was clearly a wildly amusing private joke.

"Is that—" I began to whisper to Jacob.

Before I could finish my question, Annabelle appeared on the trail. Even from this distance, I could see that she looked beautiful—dewy instead of sweaty, with her hair gathered into a charmingly messy bun on top of her head. Instead of practical shorts and sneakers like I'd worn, she was dressed in Birkenstocks and a flowy sundress.

Owen stole up behind her, put his hands around her waist, and said, "Gotcha."

Annabelle laughed and whirled around, before matter-of-factly, almost casually, planting a kiss on his lips.

My eyelids felt like roller shades that had just been snapped open. I couldn't do anything but stare as Owen's hands moved from Annabelle's waist to encircle her back. She draped her arms luxuriously over his shoulders as they kissed again. And again. And then some more.

Only then did I remember that Jacob was right next to me. When I turned back to him, he was looking down at the water, his neck splotchy.

I felt like I should say something light and breezy, like, *Get a room, right?* If I was cool, confident, sexy Annabelle, I probably would have.

But I was just awkward, embarrassed me. So all I could do was shift uncomfortably in the water. I became very aware of my tank top clinging to my skin and the way my shorts bunched up on my legs.

I felt as clumsy as Annabelle was graceful.

"Oh my God, hi, you guys!"

That was Annabelle. She must have heard the splash from

my movement. Now she and Owen were walking toward us. They were holding hands, and their mouths still looked smeary from the kissing. But they acted like everything was as normal as could be.

"What happened here?" Owen asked with a chuckle.

I squirmed, feeling like a little kid.

"You've probably noticed that it's a little hot out," I said, with a wan smile. "Well . . ."

I shrugged and splashed around in the water a bit.

"We were just getting ready to eat," Jacob said, motioning to his backpack. "Do you guys . . . want to join us?"

"Really?" Annabelle said. "I'm starving!"

"Me too," Owen said. "I didn't get any breakfast this morning."

He stole a secret glance at Annabelle. She smiled back at him, and her eyelashes fluttered.

Clearly, they'd been together—and making out—all morning. That's why they seemed so expert at it already. Meanwhile, I was so inept at this whole courtship thing, I hadn't kissed Jacob even once in an entire week!

Maybe, I thought miserably, *that's because it's not meant to be. It's just not going to happen.*

"Yeah, have lunch with us," I agreed, pulling myself out of the sticky mud.

After stepping onto dry land, I couldn't resist casting one sad glance back at Jacob. Then I added, "No reason why not."

Chapter • Fifteen

For the next couple of days, the heat wave never wavered.

Neither, for that matter, did Annabelle and Owen's PDA.

And me? I still felt awkward whenever I saw Jacob.

But when I wasn't around him—when I was just imagining him—it was a different story. I pictured myself watching sunsets with him and using the fresh cloak of darkness to kiss.

Or stealing into the kitchen supply closet to kiss.

Most of all, I reimagined our mud bath in the creek. Instead of being crashed by Annabelle and Owen, it ended in a kiss. *Plus* peaches and pimiento cheese sandwiches.

That was the best daydream of all.

Imagining all this kissing made me self-conscious around

the *actual* Jacob. I was so full of nervous energy, he probably couldn't have kissed me if he tried.

But at least I wasn't too freaked to hang out with him. We still sat near each other at nightly sing-alongs. We went on daily lake swims with other heat-weary Camdenites. And, of course, we continued to chat our way through meals.

After breakfast on day three of the heat wave, Jacob and I emerged from the dining hall, where the air-conditioning had been blasting. We both gasped at the ovenlike heat.

"This is cruel and inhumane," Jacob said, squinting at the sun. "It's only nine o'clock!"

"Ugh, it's like all the air's been replaced by steam," I said, lifting the back of my hair and fanning my neck with my palm.

"Have you been okay in the barn?" Jacob said. "What with that forge blasting on top of everything?"

I moved my hand to my forehead so I could shield my eyes while I squinted at him. His face was cutely scrunched up with concern.

"We've got a pump right outside," I assured him. "I just splash water on my face regularly. I wish I could douse my whole head, but I think my hair is crazy enough as it is."

Jacob reached over and *touched my hair*. He didn't flick at it, the way he had on our hike. This was almost a caress, one that sent tingles shooting down my spine.

It was definitely not the sort of torrid embrace I'd been imagining. But it was *something*.

Wasn't it?

Whatever Jacob's intentions, I felt that touch down to my toes. I had to look down at my feet so he couldn't see my face go all melty and quivery.

I also avoided his gaze because this was *so* not the right time or place for a first kiss. As usual, we were right out in the open, in full view of all the Camdenites slamming out of the dining hall and complaining loudly about the heat. To top it all off, my breath probably smelled like coffee and facon.

So I kept my eyes on the ground. Even when Jacob said, "I like your hair like that."

Even when he subtly but clearly took a tiny step closer to me.

Maybe if I look up at him, I thought, *he'll kiss me anyway, despite everything. Maybe he'll finally kiss me.*

But before I could work up the courage, the dining hall door swung open again. Along with a weak gust of air-conditioning came a familiar voice—

"Well, isn't *this* refreshing?"

I sighed quietly, then turned to the door. "Oh, hi, Nanny."

My grandmother walked over to us, smiling as she fanned herself with a piece of sheet music.

"Now, living in the South my entire life, you know I've seen some heat waves," she said.

"I know, I know," I said. "And this isn't anything compared to the great sizzler of '67 or something like that, right?"

"Oh no, this is right up there with the worst of 'em," Nanny said. "But I have good news and bad news about that."

"Oh?" I said. I wondered if class was canceled so we could all spend the day swimming.

"The heat's supposed to break tonight," Nanny said.

"Finally!" I cried.

"What's the bad news?" Jacob asked, mopping at his sweaty forehead with the sleeve of his T-shirt.

"It's going to break by way of a big, bad thunderstorm," Nanny said. "At least, that's what the weatherman says."

"Ooh, I like a good storm," I said, at the exact same time that Jacob said, "Ugh, I hate thunderstorms."

"Really?" I said.

"Oh, I'm not surprised by that at all," Nanny said.

Jacob turned red. Well, redder than he already was from the heat.

"Why do you say that?" I asked.

"This boy is a *thinker*," Nanny said. "Thinkers can't just relax and enjoy the big bang of a storm without *also* calculating whether the conditions are right for a tornado. They wonder if today's the day a sinkhole is going to swallow up half the neighborhood. At the very least, they're certain they left a favorite pair of shoes in the backyard."

Jacob gaped at Nanny.

"Um, that's pretty much spot on," he said. "Except I worry more about flash floods than sinkholes. But Ms. Annie, how did you know all that?"

"Your tempo," Nanny said with a shrug. "Your fingering and vibrato—I can see the wheels turning while you play. Not that you don't play magnificently . . ."

"Aw, thanks, Ms. Annie," Jacob said, looking shy. "I *am* working on the overthinking thing."

"I can see that you are," Nanny said. "Why, practically overnight, you started bending that bone between your elbow and your wrist. The rest of it will come too, darlin'!"

My eyes locked with Jacob's, and I slapped a hand over my mouth to keep from laughing.

Then Nanny turned to me.

"And you, Little Miss Blacksmith," she said. "Will I see you tonight? I'll make the popcorn."

Nanny loved thunderstorms too. I guess she was the one who'd taught me to appreciate them. When I was little, she used to come over to our house for every big storm. She'd make popcorn, the way other grandmas do before putting on an old movie. It was never microwave popcorn. It had to be made on the stove in a saucepan—a cloudy, dented pot that was pretty much used for that purpose only. Then we'd go upstairs to the hallway window seat, and Nanny would gather me into her lap. We'd watch the lightning zigzag through the sky and stare, mesmerized, as the silhouetted tree limbs waved and wobbled in the wind. We'd count the seconds between lightning flashes and thunderclaps. We'd sing songs to the rhythm of the thunder. We'd definitely eat the whole bowl of popcorn, racing to get to the half-popped kernels in the bottom of the bowl. Then we'd lick the salt off our fingers while she walked me to bed.

I realized later, when she started doing the same thing for my little brother, Carl, that the popcorn was just a trick. She made thunderstorms into a party to make sure we loved them instead of fearing them.

It had worked. To me, storms were more cinematic than sinister. They had everything you wanted in a good movie—passion and drama, volatility and conflict, and plenty of brooding rain.

So I smiled at Nanny and nodded.

"I can't promise that I won't dash outside during the storm, though," I said. "A cold rain sounds like heaven right about now."

"Absolutely not," Nanny declared. "With all these hills and those toothpicky pine trees that'll tip over you if you so much as blow on 'em? You will stay inside with me. In fact, you might want to plan on a slumber party. Make sure to bring your jammies."

"Nan-ny," I said through gritted teeth, casting a quick glance at Jacob. My grandmother talking to me about "jammies" was *so* humiliating-slash-infantilizing. (Yes, that last term I'd picked up from Annabelle.)

Nanny waved me off with a roll of her eyes.

We still had the entire sweltering day to get through. Luckily, I had something new to hold my attention in the barn. I'd decided to make my parents an iron platter—big and oval with a shallow lip. I wanted to twirl the handles to make them look like licorice twists.

I knew my mom would love using it to serve Arnold Palmers at front-porch jams. And it would show both my parents that I was sorry for the ditch that got me sent to Camden.

Talking to Jacob about the music parties might have even made me a little nostalgic for them.

Maybe, I thought as I pounded my metal out to a flat sheet, *I'll even serve the drinks at the next party.* I started imagining what it would be like to have *Jacob* at one of our jams, fiddling so hard that he broke into a sweat, then cooling off with one of the Arnold Palmers. I imagined showing him the magnolia tree out front. It was so old that some of its low, swooping branches almost touched the ground. Standing within them, we would have had the perfect cover for a kiss. . . .

"Ugh!" I groaned.

I was getting pretty sick of all these daydreams about Jacob kissing me. It clearly wasn't going to happen, so I needed to get over it.

I resolved to start obsessing over my tray instead, just as soon as I cooled off at the pump outside the barn.

On my way out, I stopped at the table where we all stashed our works in progress.

Jack had added another couple of prongs to his set of fireplace pokers, and Anthony's bocce balls were starting to look less like wobbly ostrich eggs and more like bocce balls.

The most stunning WIP was Coach's. He was making a fireplace screen of thin-stalked iron cattails, bulrushes, and even a couple of tiny frogs. It was gorgeous—as sweet and delicate as Coach was huge and brawny.

Coach lumbered over as I admired the latest addition to the screen. A wafer-thin grass blade undulated as if it had just caught a gentle breeze.

"Wow, Coach," I said. "I still can't believe *that* came out of *those*!"

I pointed at his enormous hands.

"Always expect the unexpected, Olive Oyl," Coach said with a grin. "You of all people should get that."

I laughed.

"I get it," I said. Then I headed for the door.

When I emerged from the barn, squinting in the strong sun, I found Clint and Joe already at the water pump. Joe worked the handle, while Clint held his head beneath the spigot. He hooted happily as the water ran over his red neck.

When he saw me, though, Clint immediately stepped aside and gestured me toward the pump.

"Chivalry isn't dead," I joked as I plunged my hands into the water. I wasn't about to thrust my whole head into the stream like Clint had. Without Annabelle's magical product, wet hair in this heat would definitely lead to dandelion-head. So I splashed a handful of water onto my face, then patted some onto my neck. I held my wrists under the water and even dabbed the back of my knees. But nothing worked. I was still hot. Very hot. So hot I was going to melt. I closed my eyes and took a deep breath, which only made me feel worse. The air felt like heavy cotton in my lungs.

"You know what you really need?" Joe asked from somewhere behind me.

"Hmmm?" I responded absentmindedly. I was trying to think about Popsicles. Snow angels. Penguins.

"This!" Joe shouted. Suddenly a cascade of water tumbled over my head, hitting me so hard that I fell down in the dirt. That dirt, of course, quickly turned into mud.

I gasped as cold water streamed through my hair, soaking my clothes, even trailing into my boots. I stared at Joe, my mouth open wide in shock.

This was the kind of thing the guys did to one another all the time. They pulled pranks and told jokes and said disgusting things about one another's mothers. The recipient of the ribbing laughed it off, and it was understood that he'd be the next one to pull a prank.

But they rarely included me in their games. I didn't know if they were being sexist or courteous or if it just hadn't occurred to them. And, of course, they couldn't insult my mother, because she was also Nanny's daughter-in-law. Everybody at Camden knew you didn't mess with Ms. Annie.

The real reason I thought I was often excluded from the guys' games was this—I was an outsider. Even if I'd managed to pound out that spike and a few other weighty baubles; even if the guys had gotten comfortable enough with me to resume their rampant swearing, I was still an accidental smith. I wasn't one of them.

Until now.

That pail of water might as well have been an initiation rite. And I was surprised at how happy it made me.

Physically, it saved me too. My cold, dirty shower left me feeling exhilarated and 100 percent less fuzzy than I'd felt a few minutes earlier.

I guess that was how I had the wherewithal to scoop up a gushy clod of mud and pelt it at Clint, whooping and laughing as it hit him square in the chest of his plaid shirt.

"Hey!" he yowled.

In the next instant, we were racing each other to the pump. Because I probably weighed fifty pounds less than Clint (and I was closer), I made it there first. I grabbed an empty pail, caught the last of the water coming out of the spigot, then tossed it at him.

Clint laughed so loud that I didn't hear the squeak of the pump handle behind me. That was Joe, of course, filling up another bucket. He used it to douse me.

Our splashing and shouting drew the other smiths out of the barn. Coach, Michael, Jack, and Anthony looked at one another and then at us. They were red-faced and as draggy as basset hounds. *We* were sopping wet but *very* spry.

It took them about three seconds to join in. Within a minute, we were engaged in an all-out water war. I ended up teaming up with Joe and Clint to chase the other smiths (even Coach!) with pails and mud balls. Within ten minutes, we were all soaked. We were all filthy. And were all laughing hysterically, complete with loud snorts.

That, of course, was the moment that Jacob showed up. He was carrying a tall water bottle filled with cloudy amber liquid. He stopped short of the now-muddy courtyard. He gaped at me and the other mud-slick smiths.

"Nelllll?" he said, as if he didn't quite recognize me. He looked pink-cheeked and a little sweaty, but other than that, he was perfectly clean and respectable.

I stopped myself in mid-snort and took a few steps backward, as if I would contaminate him with my grossness if I got anywhere near him.

"I brought you this drink Ms. Betty told me about," Jacob said. "It's iced tea mixed with lemonade? It's pretty much the best thing I've ever tasted."

I opened my eyes so wide, my lashes stuck to the mud on my eyelids.

"You brought me," I breathed, "an Arnold Palmer?"

"Is that what it's called?" Jacob asked. "Cool!"

Then he walked right to me, not caring about the mud that spattered his sneakers and bare legs, and handed me the bottle.

I stared at it. I couldn't have been more shocked if Jacob had given me a dozen roses.

If ever there was a gesture that deserved a thank-you kiss, it was coming to the gross blacksmithing barn, simply to bring me a cold drink.

But of course, I was more disgustingly unkissable than I'd ever been in my life.

It was so unfair, I could have cried. But what came out was laughter. Really hard, life-is-ridiculous laughter. Between hoots and hiccups, I gasped out a thank-you.

Jacob laughed too, more in bewilderment than because he got the joke.

The joke being, of course, that the more I wanted to lock lips with Jacob, the less likely it seemed that it would ever happen.

Chapter ☕ Sixteen

I t took me a long time to scrub all the mud away, but by dinner that night, I was wearing a cool, breezy sundress and looked reasonably presentable.

Not that it matters, I told myself as I sat down next to Jacob at the big green *V*. Before we could even say hello, though, the first bolt of lightning flashed outside, followed by a thunderclap that rattled the windows.

"Here we go!" said Marnie, taking a deep, shuddery breath.

"Ooh, drama," Annabelle said, clapping her hands. "I love a good thunderstorm."

"You and Nell both," Jacob said, and I flashed him a smile.

The next thunderclap, though, was scarily loud, even to me. As the lights flickered, the rain started. It came so suddenly and so hard, it was as if someone had turned on a faucet. Or more accurately, a car wash. The gushes of water obscured the windows almost completely.

Alarmed voices rippled through the dining hall like waves of water themselves, until Mrs. Teagle's voice rang out. She was standing near the room's interior door, her hands cupped around her mouth.

"Since nobody wants to go out in this rain until it lets up a bit," she called out, "I suggest we all head up to the sing-along right after dinner? If the rain doesn't come down the chimney, we'll build a fire and have a surprise treat. It involves marshmallows, y'all. And, well, chocolate and graham crackers too. Oh, heck, I just ruined the surprise."

The room filled with nervous laughter.

But Jacob wasn't one of the ones laughing.

Neither was Nanny, whom I spotted at the table next to ours. Her face looked tight with worry as she glanced my way, so I held up the little overnight bag I'd brought to dinner.

"See you after the sing-along," I called. "Don't forget the popcorn."

"Don't you want s'mores?" Nanny replied. "I'm pretty sure that's what Mrs. Teagle was alluding to so subtly."

"Of course!" I said. "S'mores followed by popcorn is pretty much the perfect slumber party menu."

"Oh, to be fifteen again with an iron stomach," she sighed.

Either due to nerves or the promise of s'mores, everyone ate quickly, then headed up to the sing-along.

I was one of the last people up the stairs. In the landing outside the great hall, Jacob was leaning against the wall. His fiddle case was tucked beneath his arm. He seemed agitated, fussing with his case's zipper.

Through the doorway, he stared at all the people finding seats and flipping through binders of sheet music. Everyone jumped when another violent thunderclap seemed to slam down on the roof, but when it subsided, they laughed.

"Don't you want to go in?" I asked him.

Jacob shrugged.

"You want to ditch, I can tell," I said with a sympathetic smile. I nodded at his fiddle case. "I get it. I bet nobody's in the lounge downstairs. You can go there and be alone, play a little."

He looked at me frankly.

"Playing sounds good," he said. "Being alone? Not so much. I could use a distraction from this storm, especially since we're surrounded by . . . what did Ms. Annie call the pine trees? Basically very tall, very heavy toothpicks?"

"Oh, she was exaggerating," I scoffed. "We've got a bunch of these tall pine trees at home, too. Not one has ever fallen on our house."

I decided not to tell him about the one that completely smushed our car a few years ago.

We tiptoed down to the lounge. It was dim, with just a few table lamps glowing here and there.

Another thunderclap made them flicker, and Jacob inhaled sharply.

"You know," I noted, dropping my bag and flopping onto a saggy love seat by the window, "we're actually committing a public service by being down here. If a tree actually does smash into the great hall, *we* can call for help!"

Jacob finally laughed as he sat on an easy chair across from me.

"I didn't know you were so, um, dark, Nell," he said.

"Oh, I don't think I am really," I said. "Just . . . practical."

"You know the person who has to stay away from the Capitol during the State of the Union speech?" Jacob said. "Just in case the whole place gets incinerated by an alien invader?"

"Oh my God, I'm obsessed with that part!" I said. "My parents make me and Carl watch the State of the Union every year. They say it's our civic responsibility. And I *try* to pay attention, but the whole time, I'm thinking of that random secretary of the interior or whoever that they pick to sit it out. What's that *like*? Do you feel like the savior of the free world, or like the girl who didn't get asked to the prom?"

"I'm thinking the first one," Jacob said. "Politicians aren't exactly humble, you know."

I laughed, then pointed at his fiddle case with my foot.

"So, are you going to play?"

"Oh, I don't know," Jacob said with a sigh. "Don't take this the wrong way, but it's kind of hard to play in front of you, you of the effortlessly rubbery forearm and the calluses that could hammer nails."

"Listen," I said. "I actually do understand in a way. I know what it feels like to want something and not know if it's possible; if you're even worthy."

"Is that how you feel about blacksmithing?" Jacob asked, sounding surprised.

My eyes widened as I realized what I'd just said—and what I'd meant. I hadn't been talking about blacksmithing at all. I'd been talking about *him*.

Now I really *did* need to change the subject.

I quickly unzipped my overnight case and pulled out my camera. I'd tossed it in while I'd packed, thinking I might take some photos by storm light.

"How about this?" I proposed. "You play, I shoot the storm. It'll be like we both have our own projects."

Jacob smiled.

"As you wish," he said.

"Are you implying that I'm bossy, Farm Boy?" I said, poking at his *Princess Bride* reference.

"That would be inconceivable," Jacob declared.

"Har, har," I said drily.

Chuckling, Jacob pulled out his fiddle and started plucking the strings to tune it. I tapped buttons and twisted dials on my camera, adjusting it for night vision. High above our heads, I could hear the sing-alongers start a mountain tune with pretty harmonies. Outside, the rain *whooshed* against the window in rhythmic gushes. It was all very cozy, which must have been why Jacob relaxed. In fact, as he got ready to play, he moved closer to the window.

"So I can see," he explained, pointing with his bow at the porch light just outside the glass.

He nestled the fiddle beneath his chin and poised his bow over the A string. Just before he started playing, though, he looked over at me and smiled.

"I'd like to think I'm more of an Inigo Montoya than the Farm Boy," he said.

I smiled.

"The guy who spent his whole life learning sword fighting to avenge his father?" I said. "Yeah, I can see that."

"Well, the first part," Jacob said. "Not so much the revenge. My dad's alive and well and probably eating nachos in front of a DVR'd UConn game right now."

"Mmm, nachos," I groaned. "With ground beef?"

Jacob snorted. Then he started playing.

I couldn't move during the first few seconds of his piece. It was one I knew, an Appalachian fugue that Nanny taught a lot. I'd always had a soft spot for it, but the way Jacob played it made it sound like something I'd never heard before. His touch was so light and airy, yet powerful.

It's possible that the way I heard Jacob's music was affected by the way I saw him. With the big window behind him, he was nothing but a silhouette. He swayed gracefully with the music. The lean muscles in his bowing arm rippled, and his hair flopped all over the place, looking way more rock star than Appalachian fiddler.

Only when I realized that he was more than halfway through the piece did I remember the camera sitting in my lap. Stealthily I picked it up, not wanting to break his concentration. I turned off my flash so I wouldn't distract him—and because I wanted to capture that silhouette against the light outside.

I started shooting. At first I focused on Jacob's bow arm, but almost without realizing it, my lens traveled upward. His face was shadowed, but even in this light, I could see it was filled with concentration and joy.

His eyes were closed, but during a big crescendo, they opened. At that exact moment, lightning flashed, making his face look exultant and, frankly, gorgeous.

I forgot to lift my finger off the shutter button, filling at least twenty frames with his face.

A moment later, like a magic spell had broken, he was done. I dropped my camera in my lap. Jacob stared at me, looking stunned and delighted.

He shook his head in wonder.

"I never played it like that all day," he said. "Not once. What did you do to make me play like that?"

"Maybe I reminded you that playing a little fiddle isn't as high stakes as fighting to the death to avenge your father," I said.

Jacob grinned at me.

"Want to hear some more?" he asked breathlessly.

"I do."

He played again. This time, I didn't shoot. I just watched.

Then I closed my eyes to listen. Then I watched some more. At some point, I kicked off my shoes and curled up on the love seat, tucking my legs under the long skirt of my sundress.

At another point, the rain seemed to shift from torrential to merely pouring, and the sing-along crowd drifted from singing to chatting to shuffling down the stairs. But I was only half-aware of it all. Even in the cavernous lounge, surrounded by doors and windows, it felt like Jacob and I were in our own little world; like nobody else existed.

Maybe *that* was why Jacob could play so comfortably.

Or maybe, I thought, *it's because he's playing for me.*

As happy as this made me, I wasn't sorry when Jacob finished his final piece and flopped down on the couch next to me.

"Wow," he said, laying his fiddle and bow on an end table. His voice was low and throaty. "That was . . . surprising."

"Camden is full of surprises," I said quietly. I wanted to turn toward him, to look him in the eyes, to make it that much more easy for him to kiss me. But I was too nervous.

"That's definitely the truth," Jacob said. His voice had gone back to normal—light and lilting. "I can't imagine anywhere else where some skinny little girl could start a water war among a bunch of blacksmiths."

I laughed.

"Oh, I love blacksmithing. Only surrounded by people like Clint and Jim and Coach could I be considered 'little.'"

"Don't you like being tall?"

"I guess," I said, shrugging. "I had a complex about it in elementary school, when I was the tallest kid in my class, girls *and* boys included. But now that most people have caught up, I don't think about it so much."

"I guess I'm glad I don't have to have a complex about being short," Jacob said. "I think I've got enough to contend with, between the glasses and the violin."

He twisted on the love seat to face me, and suddenly, I found it impossible *not* to look at him.

"I don't think there's anything wrong with glasses or violins," I whispered.

As if on cue, lightning lit up the sky and illuminated Jacob's face. His expression seemed at once determined and fearful.

I guess the determination won out, because he began leaning toward me, his head tilted to the left. The post-lightning thunder boomed nearby, but Jacob didn't seem to even hear it. Reflexively I tilted *my* head to the right, and my eyes fluttered closed. As I waited for his lips to touch mine, my heart pounded in my ears, canceling out the *whoosh-whoosh-whoosh* of the rain.

That's probably why I didn't hear, at first, my grandmother slam through the door. I also didn't hear her moans.

No, the only thing that made me open my eyes was the kiss— the kiss that never happened.

By the time my eyes had refocused, Jacob was already at the door, helping Nanny hobble inside. She was wearing her yellow raincoat, but the hood had fallen back and her face was soaked. It was also contorted in pain.

That's when I noticed Nanny cradling her left arm in her right hand.

"Where *were* you?" she snapped at me.

Chapter ● Seventeen

About an hour later, after Mrs. Teagle had taped up the middle two fingers on Nanny's left hand and I'd run to her cottage to get her some dry clothes, we were back in the lounge. Nanny was stretched out on a velvet couch the color of eggplants. Her good hand held a mug of herbal tea, her feet were covered by an afghan, and Jacob and I had turned on enough lamps that the room's thrilling shadows had been replaced by a warm, golden glow.

Now Jacob and I sat in armchairs facing Nanny. These chairs, I might add, were a good six feet apart. Wherever I aimed my gaze, I made sure it was *not* at Jacob, and I'm pretty sure he was doing the same thing.

"Nanny," I said. "I'm so, so sorry."

"Nell, stop saying that over and over," Nanny insisted. "It's done.

And besides, it's not really your fault. A misunderstanding, is all."

By "not really your fault," Nanny pretty much meant it was all my fault.

The whole time Jacob and I had been hidden away down here, Nanny had thought I was upstairs with *her*, tucked into the soprano section, warbling away while the storms raged outside.

When the sing-along broke up—and I was nowhere to be found—Nanny assumed I'd gone ahead to her cottage. She bundled herself up in her slicker, borrowed one of the lodge's big golf umbrellas, and trudged through the rain to meet me there. When she found the cottage dark and empty, she got worried and hurried back toward the lodge to try to find me.

A gust of wind that turned her umbrella inside out, a disorienting thunderclap, and a slip in the slick grass were all it took to send Nanny sprawling, spraining the middle finger of her left hand. Her fiddle-fingering hand.

And now Jacob and I were squirming with guilt.

"It's still raining," I said, my voice thin and desperate-sounding. "Do you want me to go to the kitchen and make some popcorn? I know where Ms. Betty keeps it."

"No, dear," Nanny said. "Not in the mood."

She moved her bandaged hand a bit and winced at the pain.

"All I really want is for this ibuprofen to kick in," she sighed.

Jacob jumped up and grabbed a small, round pillow from a nearby chair. He gave it to Nanny so she could rest her hand on it. While she smiled weakly at him, I growled, "I *wish* this stupid place had cell reception. You could have just called me. Then none of this would have happened."

"Or if I'd kept my head on straight," Nanny said, frowning. "But you know me and thunderstorms, Nell. I'm a wreck."

"Excuse me?" I sputtered. "No, you're a *rock*. What about all our storm-watching nights on the window seat? We always had such fun."

"Well, it was either that," Nanny said, "or I rattled around at home, jumping half out of my skin with every thunderclap."

That's when I realized what all that popcorn on the window seat had been about. Nanny had made the storms into a party for me and Carl to make *herself* less afraid.

"It became all about you," Nanny said. "I had this silly idea that if a tree ever fell on the house while I was there, I'd somehow make sure that it hit me and missed you."

"Wow, Nanny," I said. "That's sweet, in a twisted kind of way."

I sneaked a glance at Jacob and found him peeking at me, the corners of his mouth twitching. I knew *just* what he was thinking: *See, Nell? Being dark must be in your genes.*

Nanny, meanwhile, emitted a dry little laugh.

"That's just how you think once you're a parent," she said. "Even more so when you're a granny. I guess that's why I was worried about you tonight."

Normally, this would have made me indignant and embarrassed. I was fifteen! I didn't need Nanny to rescue me or take care of me. I could take care of myself!

But she looked so sweet and vulnerable and, well, *old* there on the couch with her afghan and tea. I couldn't be annoyed with her. I was just grateful she wasn't hurt worse by her fall.

"By the way, Nell," Nanny added, "Camden isn't a stupid place. It's magical."

"And I took it away from you," I said. My voice suddenly went thick, and tears sprang to my eyes. "Mrs. Teagle said you need two to three weeks to heal. By the time you can play again, we'll be home."

Nanny gazed down at the big wad of gauze on her hand.

"I can't play," she declared. "But I can still teach. Except I'll need help."

Jacob perked up, seeming grateful for something to do.

"Everyone in the class will help you," he promised. "Whatever you need. And if they try to bring in a sub, we'll boycott!"

"Oh, Jacob, bless your heart," Nanny said, smiling at him again. "But I don't think any grand rebellion is going to be necessary. All I need is someone who can play what I say. A translator, I guess you'd call it. And that someone has to know *my* musical language; has to know it very well, indeed."

I slumped down in my chair and gazed at the ceiling. I felt like a balloon being deflated, the air flowing out of me with a pathetic, whistling sound. Nanny could pretend all she wanted that she was just doing some innocent musing, but her manipulation was crystal clear.

"I suppose the *best* translator," Nanny went on, "is someone who's been speaking that language her whole li—"

"Okay," I blurted. "I get it, Nanny. I'll do it."

"You'll . . .?" Jacob looked at me, his eyebrows so high I could see them above his glasses frames.

"I'll be Nanny's assistant," I told him.

I turned to Nanny.

"So, you'll tell them what to do and I'll demonstrate how to do it?" I said.

"That's about it," Nanny said, nodding firmly and looking pleased with herself. "It's what we'd planned on anyway, remember?"

"But what about blacksmithing?" Jacob said. He was sitting on the edge of his chair now, looking concerned.

I shrugged.

"I guess I'll have to give it up," I sighed. "I'll find Coach at breakfast and let him know."

"Just follow the platter with the extra bacon," Nanny said with a smile, "and you'll find him."

Great, I thought. *So not only do I have to tell Coach I'm bailing on his class, I have to do it in front of a mound of torturously delicious breakfast meat.*

I'd been in crisis mode—shaky, guilt-racked, and high-strung—ever since Nanny had stumbled through the door.

But now that she was safe and my fate was sealed, I suddenly felt depleted and not a little depressed. I'd been trying to escape my fiddling destiny, but it had caught up with me. It would *always* catch up with me.

The fact that assisting Nanny would mean spending my days

with Jacob should have cheered me. But I'd gotten fatalistic about him, too. Surely after being thwarted so many times, he'd been traumatized out of the idea of kissing me.

Annabelle would have said the universe was trying to tell us something.

Maybe it was finally time to listen.

Chapter ● Eighteen

That night in our dorm room, I told Annabelle everything that had happened. And everything I was feeling.

"I've got emotional whiplash," I complained. "I *want* to spend every minute with Jacob. But that makes me crazy, because it's becoming really clear that things just aren't going to happen between us. So really, I should just keep my distance, right? But now, of course, I can't! Which is making me *crazier.*"

"Wow," Annabelle said as she climbed into her bed and snuggled into her pillow. "That sounds really complicated."

"Right," I said, flopping into my own bed. "And complicated is totally your area. So lay it on me, Annabelle. What should I do?"

"You should"—Annabelle's voice sounded soft and watery—"ask me in the morning? I was up too late last night."

"Were you with Owen?" I asked, trying not to let any jealous-green notes into my voice.

"Mm-hmm," she said.

"What'd you guys do?" I asked.

"Walked, talked, kissed," Annabelle said, sounding happy. "It was fun. And you know, it was all because I took your advice! Remember, you told me not to overthink it too much? To just go with it?"

I flung an arm over my forehead and groaned.

"Is that what I said?"

"Uh-*huh*," Annabelle said. "Owen and I also agreed to just enjoy this month together and deal with later, later."

"That sounds reductive," I sighed. I'd heard Annabelle use that term in the dining hall recently. "Nice and reductive."

"Um, that's not really how you use that word," Annabelle said. "I think you mean simple?"

"Don't take this the wrong way," I said, "but you have a *lot* of vocabulary words I don't get."

Annabelle laughed while I frowned at the dark ceiling, missing the glow-in-the-dark stars that were in my bedroom at home. Staring at them always helped me drift off to sleep when I was fretful.

"Hey," Annabelle said, reaching over to poke me, "that was *good* advice you gave me. Maybe it's time for you to follow it."

"You're the one who told me I should think about Jacob more!" I said, sitting up in my bed and pointing at her. I didn't care if she couldn't see me in the dark. "That I should think about kissing him. Well, I did. Think about it, I mean. To the point that I'm now a hormone-addled ball of crazy."

Annabelle turned on her side and tucked her hands beneath her cheek.

"I think you need to talk to him," she declared.

"No way," I gasped.

"Yeaaaah, you need to talk to him," she insisted.

"Seriously, I can't. What if it doesn't go well? What if I've been delusional about him liking me that way? I have to face him *every day*."

"Well, then you need to do something to take your mind off him," Annabelle said with maddening logic. "And ooh, I have just the thing. But we'll do it in the morning. Set your alarm for six."

"Six?!" I said. "Why?"

"You'll see," Annabelle said. Then she flipped over, pointedly turning her back on me. In a few minutes, her breathing slowed and it was clear she had fallen asleep.

Remembering the gross burnt sage from our first day at Camden, I was a little apprehensive about Annabelle's secret plan. And I was sure waking up two hours earlier than I normally did wouldn't make the day any easier.

But what did I have to lose by going along with her? I'd already lost blacksmithing.

And Jacob? Him, I'd never really had.

• • •

The next morning Annabelle and I left the dorm at six fifteen. She somehow looked gorgeous in a pair of Indian pajama bottoms and a tank top, her curls plaited into two loose braids.

I, on the other hand, was wearing two different flip-flops and had a bad case of dandelion head.

But at least the heat had broken as promised. The air felt cool and clean. It pepped me up and even made me feel a little optimistic.

Annabelle carried a sack made of burlap or hemp or some other earthy-smelling fabric. From it, she extracted a bottle of water and a bag of nuts.

"Breakfast," she said handing them to me before taking out her own bottle and bag. "Raw almonds and dried blueberries. Full of antioxidants."

"Does that mean we're skipping real breakfast?" I asked. "I heard Ms. Betty's making sweet potato biscuits."

"This is a cleanse," Annabelle pronounced seriously. "Sweet potato biscuits are full of processed wheat and butter."

Super-delicious *processed wheat and butter,* I grumbled in my head. Then I peered suspiciously at my water bottle.

"There's no wheatgrass or anything like that in here, is there?" I asked.

Annabelle heaved a long-suffering sigh.

"It's not *that* kind of cleanse," she growled.

"Sorry," I murmured.

Annabelle tried to make her face return to its former serene, yoga-goddess expression.

But I guess she couldn't quite *cleanse* my wheatgrass crack from her mind, because a moment later she slapped her hand over her mouth and snorted.

That made me start giggling, and soon we were both stifling shrieks of laughter.

"Here, calm down and have a raw nut," I gasped, thrusting her bag of squirrel food at her. "Yummy."

"You're a nut," Annabelle replied, grabbing an almond and pelting me with it.

Then we hurried away from campus. After a few minutes of hiking in the glow of the sunrise, I realized where we were going.

"This is the Saturn trail, the one that goes to the creek," I said.

"Uh-huh," Annabelle said. "We need running water."

I skidded to a halt.

"Not *that* running water," I said. "That creek is the exact wrong place for me to 'cleanse' myself of Jacob. Every time I picture the two of us in that creek I get . . . well, I get *very* distracted."

"Ooh!" Annabelle exclaimed happily. "That makes it an even more perfect place for this! C'mon!"

She grabbed my arm and yanked, forcing me to continue up the trail. When we arrived at the creek, it was bathed in slanting rays of sunlight. It felt so much like a magical glade, I was tempted to start turning over rocks to look for fairies.

"Wow," I breathed. "I'm usually more of a sunset girl, you know, because of my love for *sleep* and all, but this sunrise is really pretty."

"Shhh," Annabelle whispered.

"Oh, right," I said, trying not to giggle again. "Less talking, more cleansing. So what do we do?"

Ceremoniously, Annabelle pulled a slip of paper and a pen out of her bag.

"Write down what you want to cast out of your mind," she ordered.

I crouched down and pressed the paper to my knee.

Jacob, I wrote.

Then I bit my lower lip. What was I saying, exactly? The last thing I wanted was to cast Jacob out of my life. Even though we'd known each other for such a short time, he somehow already felt like an essential part of me.

But he also made me feel this unwelcome wanting. Missing. I missed him, even though he was right here.

Then I realized that what I wanted and missed wasn't Jacob himself. It was *us*—the couple we should be instead of just friends.

No matter how much I loved talking to Jacob and walking with him and even flinging soapsuds all over an industrial kitchen with him, the "just friends" thing was torturing me.

When I released my lower lip from between my teeth, I was surprised to feel it trembling. Tears prickled behind my eyes. I clenched the pencil in my fist and muttered, "#$%^."

"Whoa," Annabelle said. "Where'd you learn *that*?"

"Oh, sorry," I said, hoping she couldn't hear the tears in my voice. "That's what happens when you hang around with a bunch of blacksmiths."

"Maybe it's also what happens when a cute violinist has you in his crush clutches?" Annabelle asked, smiling at me sympathetically.

"Maybe," I said. As I smiled back at her, a tear did squeeze out of my eye and trail down my cheek. I swiped it away and looked down at my little slip of paper again.

I amended it to say, *I want to stop yearning for more with Jacob. I want to be satisfied with the way things are.*

I folded the paper into a tiny square and tried to hand it to Annabelle.

"No, no, this is *your* journey," she said.

"O-kay," I said. "So . . ."

"So, throw it in the water!" Annabelle declared. "Cast it away."

I took a breath and tossed the paper into the creek. As tiny as it was, it didn't fly very far. It landed with a plop, then caught on a rock for a moment before the water whisked it away.

It was all very unsatisfying.

"Maybe I should have made a wish or something," I observed.

"This isn't throwing a penny in a fountain, Nell," Annabelle scolded me. "It's much more meaningful. And besides, you're not done."

"Oh," I said, watching as she reached again into her burlap sack. She pulled out a necklace—a black leather thong with a tiny glass jar dangling off it.

"Now," Annabelle instructed, "open the jar and fill it with some mud and water from the creek bed."

"Seriously?" I said.

"Nelllll."

"Okay, okay," I said. I squatted at the edge of the creek and scooped up a thimbleful of brown silt and mucky-looking water. As I screwed on the top and put the necklace on, Annabelle waved something at me. I breathed in a gust of acrid smoke.

"The sage smudge!" I coughed. "I was afraid of that!"

"What? It's part of the cleansing," Annabelle insisted.

"Well, I'm cleansed enough, thank you!" I yelled.

"All right," Annabelle said. She dipped the smudge in the creek, and the flame went out with a hiss. "I hoped it wouldn't be as gross out in the open air."

"Well, it's the thought that counts," I said, giving her a quick hug. I stretched my necklace taut so I could eye my little jar of creek water and silt.

"So, let me guess," I said. "Every time I start to feel like a puddle around Jacob, I'm supposed to look at this little jar of mud and say, 'Om'? And then I'll feel better?"

"It's not mud," Annabelle said. "It's a remnant of your cleanse."

"Okay, enough with the potty humor already!" I said.

Annabelle burst out laughing and gave me a shove.

"This is serious!" she said.

When my own laughter ebbed away, I gave my "remnant" a more thoughtful study.

"It's a placebo," I noted, remembering the time I'd learned about those in my sophomore science class. There were medical studies in which some people were given a real drug, and others were given sugar pills but *told* they had the real drug. Often, the patients with the fake pills did just as well as those with the real ones, simply because they believed in them.

"A placebo? How do you figure that?" Annabelle said as she slung her bag back over her shoulder.

"It's not about the mud," I said. "Or the slip of paper. It's about what they mean to me."

"Well, that's right, I guess," Annabelle said. "So do they? Mean something to you?"

I felt grateful to Annabelle for this "journey," semi-ridiculous though it was. But I couldn't lie.

"I honestly don't know," I said. "I like the idea of them. But will they work?"

Life would be much easier if you could just will ideas into reality. If I could know that Jacob felt the same way I did.

If I could know that being together in Nanny's fiddle class would bring us closer, instead of tearing us apart.

If we could get over this "just friends" thing—and see what was on the other side.

Chapter ☻ Nineteen

I expected Nanny's class to be unpleasant.

I braced myself for that specific, flinchy pain that only happens when a fiddle string is played flat and/or screechy.

I prepared for boredom and plenty of long minutes spent gazing out the window while Nanny drilled her students.

And I resigned myself to a whole new set of sore muscles as I shifted from hauling and hammering to fingering, bowing, and clamping a fiddle between my chin and collarbone.

What I *didn't* expect was a game of badminton.

Yes, badminton.

We would have played tetherball, but Nanny cast the deciding vote.

"That's all I need is to mess up my other hand whacking

some ball around," she said. "Badminton I can handle."

"Okay, everyone," Nanny ordered the students, "gather your gear and let's hit it. And don't forget the music stands this time! Remember when we had to impale our poor sheet music on those tree branches?"

Everybody busted out in gales of you-had-to-be-there laughter. Then they loaded themselves (and me!) down with their fiddles, music stands, lunch cooler, and a badminton set that had been stashed in the corner of the little cabin where Nanny held her class. Also tossed in the corner, I noticed, were a croquet set, some beanbags, and even what looked like a pair of stilts.

"Surprise, sourpuss," Nanny said, grinning at me as she followed her students out the door. "You didn't think we just sat in that room and played scales all day, did you?"

"Um, *yeah*, sort of," I stammered, trailing after her with my arms full of picnic blankets.

"Like I said," Nanny said, "Camden is a magical place. You don't, how do you say it, 'dis' magic by doing the ordinary."

The class trooped toward the big open field behind the great lodge. It was a favorite for lawn games and picnics and lolling. As they strolled along, chatting and laughing together, I caught up with Jacob.

"So *this* is why you were desperate to get into Nanny's class?" I said. "Badminton!? How did you get all those finger cramps and calluses if you were playing *badminton*?"

"Oh, that was the first few days," Jacob said. "The hazing, we called it. Ms. Annie didn't let up until Tamara over there passed out one day."

"*What?!*" I shrieked as Jacob pointed at a girl wearing a kelly-green headband and cute capri pants.

"I'm kidding!" Jacob said with a laugh. "Although don't let Tamara fool you. She's only a high school freshman, but she's hard-core. She kicked my butt when we did hurdles."

"Your bu— *hurdles?*" I sputtered.

"Hurdles are the best!" Jacob assured me. "Especially for me. You know I'm kind of hung up on counting. But you do enough hurdles, the rhythm just kind of moves into your bones, you know. Then hopefully into your music, too. *That's* the part I'm still working on."

Then he gave me a sweet smile that filled me with a glowy feeling. I dared to think that maybe the whole silly cleanse plus mud talisman had worked. I was feeling a little better about Jacob. I realized that when I was with him, I couldn't help but enjoy his company, despite the yearning.

And despite the fact that in two weeks, he'd be returning to Connecticut and I'd be back in Georgia.

The fact was, I was also distracted from Jacob by Nanny's crazy class.

At home, my grandmother was a taskmaster. She made me memorize a new piece of music from day one, and then made me practice it ten times a day. Here at Camden, she was like Maria von Trapp and that teacher from *Dead Poets Society*, all rolled into one. Nanny was *cool*.

And the badminton lesson couldn't have been more fun.

I'd always loved the game. I loved how the shuttlecock moved in slow motion and the rackets were wispy and weightless. Badminton was a sport *made* for the non-sporty, i.e., a bunch of musicians.

Although once we got the game going, I realized Jacob was right. Tamara *was* a badass. She beat the pants off the rest of us, who included Will, a boy who'd also been playing fiddle all his life, an engaged couple in their early twenties named Shana and Harley, and Victoria, a quiet classical violin major who wanted to get her Appalachian groove on.

The game worked like this. Four players worked on the Appalachian fugue, while the remaining two played badminton. The players had to keep time with the back-and-forth of the shuttlecock *and* vice versa, all of them trying to feel their way to perfect, yet organic, rhythm. When Nanny yelled, "Switch!" the badminton players dropped their rackets and ran for their fiddles, while two of the fiddlers thrust their instruments at me (when playing fiddle/badminton, apparently, the assistant's job is handling the gear) and dashed out to the court.

And of course, we all laughed hysterically through the entire thing.

Another thing we did was duck into the trees to find the perfect echo chamber for the music. The students played facing each other and with their backs to each other, trying to infuse their playing with the breezes whispering through the leaves or with the grind of the cicadas.

It was all really, really weird. But you know what? It worked. The students' music wasn't perfect, but it had life and lilt to it. Even Jacob's.

Especially Jacob's.

His bow seemed to barely touch the strings. It was like the music was coming out of his chest or haloing around his head instead of vibrating out of his instrument. When he finished, he didn't aim his big, beaming smile at Nanny. He shone it at me.

And when we improvised a call-and-response to birdsongs, Jacob didn't close his eyes like the other students, the better to hear the distant trills and chirps. He looked at me.

Was he giving me those adoring looks because he thought I was cute, in a frizzy-haired, flat-chested, faux vegetarian kind of way? Was he falling for me?

Or was he just happy that I was finally ensnared in his earnest fiddler's world and finding that it didn't suck?

After an idyllic picnic lunch, Nanny gestured for me to help her up from the folding chair we'd brought for her.

"All right, folks," she said. "Let's head back."

There was less laughing and chatting during the walk back to the cabin. After everyone had set up their music stands inside, I found out why.

"Okay," Nanny announced. "We're going to take everything

we did out there, all that freedom, and we are going to whip it into shape. I want technique. I want precision. I want perfection. But I *also* want the breeze in the trees and the badminton. I want light and air and fun. Easy enough?"

Every face fell—while I pressed my knuckles against my lips to keep from laughing.

"You were holding out on me," I whispered to Nanny. "You're just as evil as ever."

"Don't think of it as evil," Nanny said, giving me a wink. "Think of it as scarily effective."

She began combing through the students' playing, measure by measure, sometimes note by note. Nanny led me around the room like her own personal puppet, ordering me to show Shana how to play her sequence with more vibrato, or demonstrate to Will how a phrase could become breezier.

Sometimes, of course, Nanny had to correct *me*, but she'd been instructing me for so long that I could usually figure out what she wanted with nothing more than a two-word prompt.

Before long, and without really deciding to do so, Nanny and I started teaching in tandem. While she helped Victoria smooth out her bowing, I gave Will tips on his finger work. When Tamara needed help on an intricate passage, she grabbed me because I was closer. Meanwhile, Nanny tapped Harley's music stand with her good hand to help him stay on rhythm.

But then a moment came when the most natural place for me to go was to Jacob.

He needed me too. Being in the classroom was making him think too hard again. I could practically see the wheels turning in his head, trying to be both breezy and note perfect; an artist and a technician.

I wished I could tell him that life was a lot easier when you strove for neither, like me.

But of course I didn't say that. Instead I watched him quietly for a moment before I sidled up to him and wrapped my fingers around his left wrist.

Squawwwwwwk.

Jacob's bow skittered off his fiddle strings with such force that I had to duck to avoid a poke in the eye. Once I was crouched on the floor, it took a moment of heavy breathing before I could get up again. Apparently, that was what happened to me when I touched Jacob, even on the wrist.

Jacob, too, looked winded and his neck had blotched right up.

"$(#@, I'm sorry," he whispered, ducking down to help me up.

"$(#@?!" I whispered back with a giggle. "Clearly you've been hanging out with a few too many blacksmiths."

"Maybe one in particular," Jacob said. "You're a bad influence, what can I say?"

You could say that you like *my bad influence,* I thought, pining. *Then you could toss your fiddle on the table and take me out to the woods, where we could make out like mad.*

My inhale was shuddery and little sad before I said, "Anyway, I was just trying to get you to drop your wrist. I think that would loosen up your trill, loosen up everything, really."

"Along with the flexible forearm?" Jacob said skeptically.

"Yup," I said, trying not to sound bored by this discussion of fiddle technique. "Everything loose, everything easy."

"Yet every note perfectly in tune and right on the beat," Jacob said, shaking his head.

"Yup," I said again, laughing this time. "Simple."

Jacob shrugged and tried my wrist-dropping trick. But that made him forget to loosen his bow arm. When I corrected that, his wrist crept up again. That's when Nanny sauntered over and watched Jacob play for a couple of measures.

"I think this is a wrist issue," Nanny said, squinting at Jacob's left hand. "You need to drop it a little and . . . Nell, show him what I mean."

Shooting Jacob an apologetic glance, I picked up my own fiddle and played the passage with my wrist low and my limbs loose. The music was as light and fast as a bird's wing.

"See!" Nanny said. "Simple. And impossible, I know, darlin'. But just keep working at it. One day—*click*—it's gonna be right there, and you'll thank me for all this torture."

Jacob gave Nanny a sheepish smile. She headed over to Victoria, but I stayed put.

"You know I totally hate you right now," Jacob whispered to me.

"I'm sorry!" I whisper-wailed.

He laughed and cringed all at once.

"Don't be," he said. "You can't help it if you're a ridiculously talented Finlayson, any more than I can help being . . . whatever I am."

"You're a fiddler, Jacob," I said fiercely. "A real one. Please don't doubt that. So yeah, you didn't have what I had growing up. But you've got so much passion. And, hello, you're here! You're learning every day."

"You're right," Jacob said, gazing at the floor. "I just wish sometimes that it didn't have to be so hard to get what you want."

Since his eyes were downcast, I allowed my gaze to linger on his shiny hair, his beautifully imperfect nose, his sharp jawline.

"Believe me," I whispered. "I know exactly what you mean."

Chapter ● Twenty

ere was another thing Nanny hadn't told me about her fiddling class. On the second-to-last day of the session, they got to escape from Camden!

Of course, Nanny didn't refer to it as an escape. She called it a field trip.

We left early in the morning, all of us piling into Camden's big, clunky, forest-green van. We were headed for Asheville, about an hour's drive from the school.

My family went to this little North Carolina city often to play concerts. It was one of my favorite places on earth.

On one hand, it was a cute, small town tucked away in the mountains—the kind of place you go to get *away* from the big city. But in many ways, Asheville was more urban than Atlanta.

Where Atlanta sprawled, overrun with strip malls, downtown Asheville was packed densely with walkable streets and plazas, and awesome, quirky shops topped by lofts. It was filled with artists and musicians, many of them just a few years older than me. Rent was cheap in Asheville, so they were free to prowl the sidewalks, making renegade public art.

That's why we were going there. Nanny (I'd learned) subjected all her Camden students to the Busking Test. They had to play on various street corners and see if they could hack performing for random strangers.

When we made it down from Camden's mountain, I couldn't stop myself from whooping with joy. I turned my face toward the open window, grinning as the wind did its best to breeze through my hair. (In honor of my return to civilization, I'd flatironed my less-black-than-ever bob and sprayed it into submission. I was also wearing one of my favorite shreddy tank tops and a miniskirt.)

"I have permits for each of you," Nanny announced, passing back a stack of stapled papers, "as well as maps of all the places busking is authorized in the city. So if the police hassle you, you can just produce your paperwork."

"Ms. Annie," Victoria said breathlessly, "you make it sound like we're planning a caper instead of just playing fiddle on the sidewalk."

"*Just* playing fiddle on the sidewalk?" Nanny gasped. "Vicki, nothing's more badass than busking."

"Nanny!" I gasped. "Did you just use the word 'badass'?!"

"Sorry, sweetheart." Nanny shrugged. "There's really no other word for busking. It's not for the faint of heart. To start with, you don't have a captive audience who've bought tickets to your recital and *have* to be polite. Passersby are brutally honest. You play something that hooks 'em, they'll stop and give you two precious minutes of their time. If you *really* wow them, they'll drop a dollar into your fiddle case. But it's also good if people tell you you're noise pollution. That shows you made an impression."

"Insults are good?" Jacob asked from his seat next to mine.

"Oh, yes," Nanny said, nodding hard. "That's why I harass *you* people every day. The only thing I don't want to hear about is indifference. If someone walks right by you without noticing you're there? Well, that means you're background noise. You're the wallpaper. And you all have too much personality for that."

After we arrived, Harley parked our mortifying short bus in a parking deck. We all grabbed our fiddles and stumbled out to the sidewalk.

"It feels so . . . crowded," Shana said, clutching her violin case tightly. A small pack of people sauntered by, all of them proudly wearing that skinny, scruffy, sleepy-eyed look of college kids on summer break. One of the girls had teal hair and chipped black nail polish. The guys all wore T-shirts advertising bands that nobody had heard of yet. Their hair looked like their girlfriends had given them DIY trims with razor blades. They were so impossibly cool, I couldn't help but stare.

I sneaked a glance at Jacob to see if he was playing it cooler than I was. But he had the exact same stargazey, yearning look on his face. It made me want to throw my arms around him and bury my face in his neck.

I didn't do that, of course. I *couldn't* do that. But I did hazard a smile at Jacob, a big, geeks-like-us grin.

Meanwhile, Harley spotted a chain coffee shop across the street about a block away.

"Shana!" he said, squeezing her arm.

"Ooh!" she cried, clapping her hands. "We are going over there *right now*."

"She's been moaning about missing her precious soy lattes ever since we got to Camden," Harley confided to the rest of us. Shana laughed and punched his arm.

"I could go for a Frappuccino," Tamara piped up. Murmuring in agreement, the group began to walk toward the shop. But I hesitated.

Coffee chains made me itchy. They were well lit and easily wipe-downable. The baristas wore green visors. *Everybody* had heard of the bands on their sound system.

"I wonder if they'll have pumpkin flavoring, even though it's summer?" Shana said.

Jacob held back with me, and once again, we exchanged a secret smile.

"I have a feeling that you think pumpkin soy lattes are a crime against nature," he whispered.

"Not against nature so much as against coffee!" I said, curling my lip.

"This from the girl who likes her coffee white," Jacob teased me.

"Beige!" I protested. "You can still taste the coffee under the milk. Faintly. How did you know how I drink my coffee anyway?"

"Do you know how I take mine?"

Without hesitation, I said, "Black, half a teaspoon of sugar."

"See?" Jacob said. "I don't know if you've noticed, but we've been having breakfast together for a while now."

I felt the same way I had that first morning Jacob saw me in a swimsuit—revealed.

But not necessarily in a bad way.

"Anyway," Jacob went on, "I'm not feeling much like coffee right now. I'd rather eat."

"Want an early lunch?" I proposed, glancing at my phone. "It's eleven thirty. If we eat now, we'll be hungry again before we head back to Camden, and we can get some gelato."

"You know," Jacob said, as we crossed the street, "to look at you, you would never guess how obsessed you are with food."

"I'm only obsessed when I've been subsisting on a diet of meat-free casseroles," I said.

"Well, I'm obsessed all the time," Jacob admitted. "But I'm a guy. We're universally acknowledged to be pigs. Most girls are all about the salads."

"I guess I'm different from most girls," I said with a shrug.

"You're singular," Jacob said.

"What?"

"You said that to me once," he said. His neck started to go blotchy, and he avoided my eyes. "When I called you 'y'all.' You said, 'I am singular.' I've got to say, I agree."

"Singular" doesn't seem like a compliment. After "smart," most girls would probably prefer "pretty" or "bubbly" or "hot."

But "singular" made me swoon. Once again, I had that urge to throw myself at Jacob.

Instead I hurried over to Nanny, who was holding the coffee shop door for the other students.

"Well," she mused, "I suppose as long as we're here I might get myself a grande macchiato with an extra shot and a caramel drizzle."

"Nanny!" I said. "How many more times are you going to shock me today?"

"Sweetie," Nanny said, "exactly how old do you think I am?!"

"You are fabulously youthful," I said, giving her a quick hug. "But you are old-*fashioned*."

Nanny let the door fall closed after the last of the fiddlers had gone inside. She gave me a tilt-headed squint.

"You know," she said, "a person who likes old music isn't necessarily old-fashioned."

She glanced at Jacob, who was standing a few feet behind me, his hands dug into his shorts pockets, his neck unblotching slowly.

"That was one of the things," Nanny said, her voice low, "that I hoped you'd learn at Camden."

"I—" I began, "I mean I—"

I didn't know what to say, except that it was kind of hard to change a major cornerstone of your worldview while standing in the doorway of a coffee shop.

And on an empty stomach.

"I . . . think Jacob and I are going to skip the coffee," I said. "We're going to get something to eat instead. Then we'll find a spot to play."

Nanny's smile was sweet and open.

"That's fine," she said. "Have fun, sweetheart. Since our phones work here, I'll call you if I have any problems with this fancy camera of yours."

Nanny patted my camera bag, which was slung over her shoulder. She'd asked to borrow it so she could shoot everyone while they were busking.

I gasped and slapped my back pocket. I'd gotten so used to my phone not working at Camden that I'd almost forgotten it was possible to make calls on it instead of just using it as a clock.

"Yeah, call me if you need anything," I said, pulling my phone out. "But I've got the camera all set up for you on auto-everything, especially auto-focus. You should be good, even with one hand."

"Okeydoke," Nanny said. "Oh, and Nell. For your busking, I recommend that you go to the corner of Wall Street and Battery Park Avenue. It's perfect for you."

"Wall Street and Battery Park," I murmured, pulling my map

and permit out of my other pocket. "Okay, why not? See you later, Nanny."

And then, because she'd been cool about me ditching the group—with a boy—I gave her another hug. I reached to open the coffee shop door for her, but she waved me away.

"You've been very helpful, Nell, since—" Nanny lifted her splinted hand and frowned at it. "I know it hasn't been easy."

"None of this has been easy," I admitted quietly. I glanced over my shoulder at Jacob. "But a smart lady once told me that nothing worth doing was easy."

I wondered if Nanny knew what I was really talking about.

"That woman was a genius," she said, "whoever she was. Now go get yourself a cheeseburger, Nell. You look too skinny, and you're definitely not fooling *me* with that silly vegetarian act."

Jacob heard that bit and didn't stop laughing until we were half a block down the street.

"I'm glad you find me so amusing in my anemic state," I said.

"Nell . . ." Jacob suddenly stopped walking and turned toward me. I felt a swoop in my belly.

"Yes?" I said. It came out squeaky.

"I want to. . . ," Jacob said hesitantly, "I want to buy you that cheeseburger."

Okay, *not* the romantic declaration I'd been expecting.

"You're not serious," I said, giving him a shove.

"I'm as serious as a fried chicken leg," Jacob said.

I flushed as we resumed walking. It seemed weird that

whenever Jacob made a gallant gesture toward me, it involved *meat*. But I'd take it.

"God, that seems like a long time ago, doesn't it?" I said. "That night in the kitchen?"

Jacob pointed at my palm, where my smooth pink scar was already starting to fade away.

"It seems like we've known each other for longer than a few weeks," Jacob said quietly. "That's for sure."

"Jacob," I said haltingly. I was on the verge of asking him how he felt about me.

Or just telling him how *I* felt about *him*.

I would rather risk extreme embarrassment than not know what this thing was between us.

"I—"

My voice literally caught in my throat. I couldn't speak! Clearly, my body was saving me from myself.

Meanwhile, Jacob had spotted a café.

"Here's a place that smells burger-y," he said.

"What?!" I asked breathlessly.

"Look," Jacob said, pointing through the window. The walls of the restaurant were wood-paneled, and the tables were draped in red-and-white-checked oilcloth. Right up front, two burly guys were eating. One was shoving a fistful of fries into his mouth, while the other hoisted a massive burger. As he took a bite, some bloody-looking juice dripped onto his plate.

There was no *way* I was eating one of those in front of Jacob.

Besides, the homespun look of this place reminded me too much of Camden.

I did a slow circle to see what else was nearby. I froze when I spotted an awning on the other side of the street. It was bedazzled with bright pink, green, and orange swirls. Through the big plate-glass window, I could see rows of sleek wooden booths, brightly colored wall tiles, and mod elephants dangling from the ceiling. On the awning was a single word: CURRY.

"I want *that*," I declared to Jacob, already stepping off the curb, "way more than I want a burger."

"What's that?" Jacob said. "Indian food? Sure, I like Indian food."

"Not just Indian food," I said, almost skipping as we crossed the street. "Indian food in a completely cool, completely *urban* restaurant. In short, everything that the Camden School *isn't*."

Chapter ●Twenty-One

We trotted over to Curry's glass door and peered through.

"The food's going to be spicy and exotic," I whispered to Jacob. "It will definitely not involve condensed soup. I can't wait!"

When we went inside, a waitress with too many tattoos to count told us to sit wherever. We rushed to grab the last table by the front window so we could watch Asheville's hipsters, hippies, and slackers lope by.

We tucked our fiddle cases safely between our chairs and the window while we read the menu.

"I don't even recognize half these things," I said happily. "Look, they have lime rickeys! I've always liked the sound of a lime rickey, but I've never had one. Limmmmme rickey!"

I was acting like a goofy tourist, but I didn't care. In fact, I loved that I could do that in front of Jacob, who one-upped me by saying, "I'm gonna have a mango lasssssssi!"

Then we laughed so hard we both flopped over on the table.

After we'd ordered *chaat*, *pakoras*, and *thalis*, we gazed out the window.

We were prepared to admire cool Ashevillians, but after a couple of minutes (and the discovery that a lime rickey was even more fabulous than I'd imagined), someone started looking at *us*. It was a little girl, maybe six years old. She was young enough, anyway, to stare and point at us while tugging on her mom's skirt.

"Um, I know we're not from around here, but do we stand out that much?" Jacob murmured.

"Yeah, I thought I looked pretty local," I said, frowning at my outfit.

When I looked back at the girl, I realized she wasn't pointing at us but at our fiddle cases. Then she jumped up and down and clasped her hands in front of her, shaking them at her mom.

"She's begging for violin lessons," Jacob said.

"You think?" I asked, surprised.

"Oh yeah," Jacob said, popping a bite of kale *pakora* into his mouth. "I spent a year doing the exact same thing when I was little."

I smiled at the girl and waved at her. She got pink in the cheeks and grabbed her mom's hand, dragging her down the street.

"Aw, we should head in that direction after lunch," I said. "I think that's where Nanny told us to go anyway. It'd be so cute to play for her. Mmm, I wonder if I should get another lime rickey to take with us."

Jacob looked at me and shook his head.

"So you never get nervous?" he asked. "About performing?"

I shrugged and tore into a piece of naan.

"I guess not," I said.

He stared out the window.

"I got such a rush right then," he said. "I was all, 'Hey, that kid thinks we're *real* musicians. Wow!' But maybe you're a real musician when you stop thinking things like that."

He turned to look at me, his smile a little sad.

"*You're* the real musician," he said. "Ironic, isn't it?"

"Jacob," I said. "What does that mean, anyway? You make music. You care about music more than anything else in the world. What's more real than that?"

Jacob's face changed then, in a way I couldn't quite interpret. He looked into my eyes.

"I care about other things too," he said quietly.

I stared back at him. Was he saying what I thought he was saying? At a moment when we were literally on display in a picture window? Where kissing absolutely couldn't happen? And when, by the way, we were only a couple of days away from saying good-bye?

I broke eye contact with Jacob, gazing into my lap as these thoughts tumbled around my mind.

"We'd better get going," Jacob said, taking another quick bite of food. "I want to start this busking business before I chicken out."

I swallowed hard and nodded while I motioned to our server for the check.

A few minutes later we'd finished eating. (Well, Jacob had done the bulk of the eating. I'd sort of lost my appetite.) We got to-go refills on our lime rickeys, hoisted our violin cases, and headed for the door.

Did he say what I thought he said? I asked myself again. I'd been at this guessing game with Jacob for so long, I didn't trust myself to answer.

I could only hope.

We followed our map, stopping along the way to peek into cool boutiques, an amazing bookstore, and a spice shop where we got to taste sea salt flavored with chocolate and wine.

When we found the spot Nanny had told me about—a small courtyard at the intersection of a couple of cute, narrow streets—I burst out laughing. Plunked in the middle of the little plaza was the most tremendous feat of blacksmithing I'd ever seen. It was a shining, black, eight-foot-tall clothes iron, tipped onto its back end. The back end of the handle touched the sidewalk, creating a perfect perch for little kids to climb. Two giggling girls were crawling on it when we arrived. The bottom of the iron cast a neat triangular shadow onto the concrete.

It was the perfect place for busking.

We unpacked our fiddles and placed Jacob's open case near our feet. I pulled out my wallet and fished out a few dollars to toss into it.

"Peer pressure," I explained to Jacob, making him laugh.

Since he was the student, he picked our playlist.

"How about we start with 'Do You Love an Apple?'" he proposed.

"Sure."

We launched into the piece, with me playing harmony to Jacob's melody. In my head, I sang the lyrics. I knew Jacob was doing the same, as Nanny required.

But these lyrics were the last thing I needed running through my head.

Do you love an apple?
Do you love a pear?
Do you love a laddie with curly brown hair?

I glanced at Jacob. His hair, in the humid almost-July air, was wavy enough that you could almost call it curly.

And still, I love him, the next line of the song went.

I can't deny him.
I'll be with him wherever he goes.

And that was just the first verse! I was sure I was turning bright red. I definitely couldn't look at Jacob. It made staying on the same beat challenging, to say the least.

Where're the songs about black lung or poisonous snakebites when I need them? I lamented silently.

Clink.

The sound of coins hitting coins startled me. I hadn't even noticed that we had a small audience. Well, it was a tiny audience of four people, all of them gray-haired and smiling at us. I could tell they thought we were cute.

But I supposed I didn't mind being cute if they were paying us for it. I gave them a little bow to thank them for the money. Then I glanced at Jacob.

He was positively beaming. And his playing was speeding up, going from sweetly romantic to a happy little jig.

It took all the awkwardness out of the love song. By the end, we were playing it twice as fast as it was meant to be. We were almost racing.

And somehow I knew this was going to be the most fun I'd *ever* had busking.

We played for at least another twenty minutes before we paused.

"This is awesome!" Jacob whispered as another spectator tossed a dollar into his case. "Even those moments when nobody's watching are cool. Because then I'm trying to *attract* listeners, which is probably even harder than keeping them once they get here."

"I never thought of that," I said. "You're right."

"So what do we do now?" Jacob said. "We've played all the

fiddle songs I know. I could do some classical stuff. Or should we just start over again with 'Do you Love an Apple?'"

"No!" I said, way too quickly.

Jacob squinted at me, confused.

"I mean . . . why not do something *really* new? Let's jam."

"Jam?" Jacob looked even more confused.

"You know," I said, "improvise. Just pretend this is my front porch."

I nodded at the giant clothes iron.

"That's the magnolia tree," I said. "And your lime rickey is now an Arnold Palmer."

"But you don't like your front-porch jams," Jacob said.

"Maybe," I ventured, "I just haven't been playing with the right people."

And then, because saying something so overt almost sent me into a panic attack, I started playing.

My improv began with a two-string shuffle, a standard fiddler's rhythm, in the key of D. I had no idea where I was going to go with it.

But when Jacob jumped in, I realized I didn't have to know. He was taking the lead. I began harmonizing to his melodies, tracking the sway of his body, the tilt of his bow, and the flash in his eyes.

Before long, this communication—part ear, part intuition—began to go both ways. Jacob followed my lead as much as I followed his.

I'd done this so many times at our jams at home, spotting the raised eyebrows or the subtle elbow swing of the other players and using that cue to take the music in a new direction. But it had never felt like this. It was like Jacob and I were talking without talking; like he knew what I was going to do a moment before I did and vice versa.

It was instinctive and exciting and . . . well, it was a lot like kissing.

But without, alas, any actual kissing.

We weren't the only ones who thought our busking was pretty amazing. As soon as we began improvising, the coins and bills really started pouring into our fiddle case. They came from the parents of little kids who danced to our songs and from more gray-haired folks who thought we were charming.

But it was when we got applause from a handful of hipsters in ironic T-shirts that Jacob and I knew we'd arrived.

Of course, we completely ruined the moment by high-fiving and jumping up and down. The cool kids rolled their eyes and marched away, but we didn't care.

"That was incredible," Jacob said to me, his eyes shining.

"*We* were incredible," I said.

He took a step closer to me.

I tilted my face upward.

He'd just started to lean down when my grandmother's voice called to us from across the street. What *was* it with her timing?!

"Oh, kids, that was amazing!" she said, hustling toward us. "Jacob, I'm so proud of you. You let go!"

"Did you hear that key change in the second half?" Jacob asked, turning away from me and grinning at Nanny. "You taught us that in week one! I don't know how it came back to me!"

"All that practice paid off," Nanny said, squeezing Jacob's arm with her good hand. She placed my camera case on the ground as she went into teacher mode. "Now, you still have to watch your wrist. And I want you to play me that part where you went *dee, dee, DEE, dee*. Remember? That was really special. . . ."

While Nanny and Jacob chattered, I slumped against the giant flatiron, feeling my heartbeat gradually slow. Between the music and the almost-kiss, it had been *racing*. Now, as the adrenaline of the moment drained away, I felt as limp as a rag doll. I slid down the smooth, cool metal of the sculpture until I was cross-legged on the sidewalk. With nothing else to do, I pulled out my camera to peek at the photos that Nanny had shot.

Squinting at the small screen, I found Nanny's first images. They were of Tamara and Victoria, hamming it up as they played together on a street corner. Then it was Will looking serious and studious on another. Shana and Harley's photos alternated between them playing blissfully together and arguing. It made me laugh because they completely reminded me of my parents.

And then, I clicked on a photo of me and Jacob.

Of us.

Of us gazing into each other's eyes while we played.

There were also shots of us with our eyes closed while we communicated only through rhythm and tone.

There were some frames featuring the hipsters dancing in circles with their arms linked; of them tossing coins into our cases.

Finally, there were a few photos of me and Jacob both looking completely and simply happy, absorbed in our music.

Or maybe we were absorbed in each other.

But what could we do about it if we were? My grandmother was here, and after that, we'd be back in a van full of people. Then it'd be the dining hall and the sing-along. We'd be surrounded at all times.

What's more, we were all heading home the day after next. Our time left together was so fleeting, you could count it down by the hour.

It's too late, I thought miserably. I turned my camera off, and the image of me and Jacob—like an alternate reality that would never come to be—went black.

Chapter ●Twenty-Two

The next morning I woke up early, my mind busy playing and replaying my day in Asheville with Jacob.

Annabelle stirred.

I turned on my side to find her staring up at the ceiling, just as I'd been. Her top sheet was twisted in her slender fingers. I wasn't the only one awake and obsessing.

"Owen?" I asked.

She didn't look at me as she nodded.

"Jacob?" she said.

"Oh yeah," I sighed. "Are you sad to be leaving him?"

"Yes," Annabelle said immediately. "And no. I mean, my next phase? College? It's all about freedom. About studying and traveling and dating and not dating and definitely not being tied down by someone who lives thousands of miles away. I want that free-dom! I do. But then I think about Owen and . . . I don't. I wonder what it might be like if I wasn't going to Brown or he wasn't going to Berkeley."

"Maybe it would have been easier," I said, propping myself on my elbow, "if you guys hadn't gotten together at all?"

"*Definitely*," Annabelle said with a sigh. "Nell, I'm going to *cry* on my plane trip home tomorrow. I'm probably going to think about Owen every other minute for a long while. I might think about him *forever*. It's really going to make it hard to write my feminist theory thesis. It was going to be all about the rise of the new Amazon."

I covered my mouth until Annabelle laughed, authorizing me to let out my own giggle.

Then Annabelle did something equally unexpected. She said, "But you know what? I don't regret a thing. I'd do it all over again."

She got out of bed and stepped over her suitcase, which was open on the floor and already half-filled. As she headed for the bathroom, I stayed in bed. I listened to the water pipes groan as Annabelle turned on the shower. I heard her say good morning to one of our other dorm mates.

I stared at the ceiling and pictured Jacob's face. I pictured his hair, too long now after a month at Camden. The dark tendrils of his bangs kept flopping over his glasses. His pale skin had turned ruddy early in the month, and now it was golden. He was maybe a little skinnier than he'd been when I'd first met him, which only made the muscles in his arms and legs pop more.

He had new freckles.

He had a smile that lit up his whole face.

I didn't know if I could bear to look at that face for six hours on this, our last day of class. Not when we'd be leaving each other so soon.

And not when so much had—and hadn't—happened between us.

I rolled out of bed and shuffled to the closet. I dug into the bottom of the badly folded stack of clothes on my shelf. I found a plain ribbed tank top and a pair of long cargo shorts. I tossed them onto my bed and grabbed a handful of hair clips off my dresser before heading to the bathroom.

If I hurried, I could make it to Nanny's cottage before breakfast and explain why I wouldn't be showing up at breakfast, or at our last class.

I was tentative when I pushed through the big barn doors. But as soon as they spotted me through the gloom, the blacksmiths treated me like their long-lost sister.

Clint whooped and rushed over to give me a hug that left sooty fingerprints on my upper arms and squeezed all the breath out of me.

Coach grinned at me so hard, his eyes disappeared into his bushy brows.

"What brings you back to the barn, Olive Oyl?" he boomed.

"Well, I never did finish that platter I was making," I said. "And I missed the beast!"

I pointed at the forge. Michael was pumping away at the bellows to liven up the fire. He waved at me between pumps, seemingly oblivious to the great gusts of heat that poured over him through the forge's open door.

"So it's okay that I'm here?" I asked Coach. "I don't want to get in your way."

"Please, you're welcome here," he boomed. "Anytime, my dear. Anytime."

I found my platter, looking dirty, crooked, and pretty pathetic, under a pile of the other guys' work. Their pieces were beautiful, even the horseshoes.

I knew there was no chance that my platter would be pretty. I just wanted to finish it before I left.

Even more than that, I wanted somewhere to hide. In the barn, my flushed face could be explained away by the two-thousand-degree fire in the forge. Tears would just blend in with the sweat. And the jangle of hammer on iron would drown out my thoughts.

At first it worked. As I struggled with my tongs and pounded my lava-colored platter, all I could think about was trying not to incur any more scars.

But then I got back into the rhythm of the ironwork—the loop from fire to hammer to hissing water bath to fire again. I luxuriated in those moments of rest, when my piece was heating up in the forge. I felt that familiar, incredulous zing as my tray thinned out further and even took on a respectably oval shape. I loved the way my hammer made a pattern of dents in the iron, a substitute for my fingerprints.

Mostly, I rocked out to the dissonant sounds of the barn: the different notes we all made with our hammers, the offbeat rhythm of our clangs, thunks, and hisses, and the rise and fall of the guys' chatting, joking, and, of course, swearing.

I was almost dancing to it.

"Look at Olive Oyl," Clint called out. "She missed us so much, she's doing a happy dance."

Okay, I guess I *was* dancing to it.

"Don't you guys hear all that?" I said. "It's like music."

Then I froze.

My arm dropped to my side, and I narrowly missed clocking myself in the kneecap with my hammer. I slowly put it down on my anvil and drifted over to one of the dirty barn windows, which was propped open with a worn-out dowel. I gazed at the long grass and shriveling, late-June wildflowers outside. They rippled in a breeze, filling my ears with rustling and just a hint of a crackle.

I looked at the gravel path and realized that all summer long, I'd been *crunch-crunch-crunch*ing through those rocks with a beat.

I hear music everywhere, I thought.

It was such a basic fact about myself, and so true, that I

couldn't believe I hadn't realized it before. All this time, I'd been fighting my birthright, reluctantly playing my fiddle, and taking music completely for granted. But all this time, I'd also been hearing music in everything, constantly.

Almost gasping, I hurried over to Coach, who happened to be admiring my platter.

"Nellie!" he said. I couldn't help but smile. He only called me that when my work bore no evidence of Olive Oyl's noodle arms. "This is good! You just need to give it a good file and buff and you're good to go."

"I'll totally do that," I said breathlessly, "but I just realized— There's this thing—"

What was I supposed to say to my teacher? *I've just had an epiphany about my entire identity, and I have to go tell the boy that I'm pretty sure I love?*

Instead I just blurted, "I'll be back!" and made a break for it.

I tried not to burst dramatically through the barn doors— but failed.

Then I tried not to gasp even more dramatically when I saw Jacob running toward the barn.

Yeah, failed at that, too.

"What are you doing here?" I said when he reached me, looking wild-eyed.

After bending over at the waist to catch his breath, Jacob looked up at me and said, "You didn't come to class. Or breakfast. But also . . . I think I just realized something."

"So did I," I said. Somehow I was just as breathless as Jacob, though I'd only run a few yards.

He straightened up, and I noticed something in his hand. It looked like a wadded-up napkin.

Following my gaze, Jacob rolled his eyes.

"Oh man," he said. "I brought you this, and then I went and squashed it while I was running."

Gingerly he peeled back the napkin to reveal a cinnamon-scented mush of bread and frosting.

"Ms. Betty made cinnamon rolls," Jacob explained. "I know they're your favorite."

"What, no steak? No pork chop?" I complained with a grin.

Jacob laughed again and moved closer to me, looking adorably awkward as he wrestled with what to do next.

I think he wanted to kiss me.

No, I knew he did. Finally. I knew.

And I wanted to kiss him.

I also wanted to tell him everything that had just raced through my mind. And listen to everything that had raced through his.

But it was very possible, after my ridiculously girly exit, that most of the blacksmiths were peeking at us through the window.

"Can we take a walk?" I asked Jacob.

"Definitely," he said.

Without discussing it, we headed in the same direction—up

the hill toward the Saturn trail. We were headed for the creek where our first kiss might have been.

Of course, I thought, shaking my head, *I could say that about so many parts of Camden.*

I'd imagined myself and Jacob—myself *with* Jacob—everywhere here. I could never separate this place from him.

The silence between us as we walked wasn't uncomfortable, but it wasn't easy, either. It crackled with longing and anticipation and anxiety.

I found I had to focus on putting one foot after the other, on swinging my arms, on breathing.

Luckily, the walk was short. We made it briefer still by walking fast. I exhaled hard when we reached the creek. Now, in the height of the summer, it was less lush. The water was lower, and the dirt next to it looked dry and sandy. The cicadas hiding in the trees sounded agitated and shrill.

Still, we sat down there, side by side. I dug my boot heels into the sand and gazed at the water, burbling over the rocks.

"Okay, you first," I said to Jacob.

"No, you," Jacob insisted.

"Well . . ." I felt nervous, of course. But unlike all those other moments that I'd let slip away, I was determined. "It's kind of a two-parter."

Jacob smiled. "We've got time."

Except that wasn't really true. There was hardly any time at all. The knowledge made a lump rise in my throat, but I willed it away. There was definitely no time for that.

I tucked my feet beneath me so I was perched on my knees. The things I wanted to tell Jacob seemed too momentous to say while sprawled comfortably in the sand.

"Well, first," I began, "music. I've realized that it's just like what you said. It *is* in my blood. It's in my *bones*. I can't get away from it, and I don't think I want to. Not anymore."

Jacob's eyes went wide.

"But my family's music?" I went on. "The old-timey, preservation stuff? The Appalachian dances and the front-porch jams that are basically endless variations on a theme? *That's* not me. What I want to do is make my *own* music. Write my own songs."

"That sounds amazing," Jacob said. "But Nell, are you sure? You're not just doing this for your grandma, are you? Or—"

He hesitated, but clearly he was feeling the same urgency I was. He didn't want to waste time being shy, worrying about the right moment or the right thing to say.

"Or for me?" he said.

I smiled big and giddy. Telling Jacob about this freshly hatched decision made it real, somehow. I'd never before felt this excited about an idea—especially a *musical* idea.

Jacob was looking pretty glowy too.

"It's not *for* you," I assured him. "But I'm pretty sure it was inspired by you."

Jacob's eyes widened.

"No, that's not right," I said, putting a finger on my lips and frowning in thought. "It's more like, like you're the glasses I didn't think I needed."

"Oh, you smug people with twenty-twenty vision," Jacob murmured.

I laughed.

"I just mean, you helped me see things differently, things like music and my family and even myself."

I put a hand on Jacob's knee and whispered, "How did you do that?"

Jacob inhaled sharply and stared at my hand—my anvil-scarred, short-nailed hand—as if it was the most beautiful thing he'd ever seen.

Maybe it was.

"I've been so dumb," he said. "How could I have thought that we should just be friends? When every day, every *moment*—especially this one—all I've wanted to do is kiss you."

The burst of energy that had brought me up to my knees suddenly left me, like a lightbulb flaming out after a power surge. I slumped down to my backside and braced myself with my hands, my stomach fluttery.

"I wanted Camden to be all about my training, my music," Jacob explained to me. "The stakes felt so high, and I worried that you'd be a distraction. And then there was the way you felt about music and the fact that we live so far away from each other. Well, it just seemed impossible."

"And now it's even more impossible," I said. "We leave tomorrow morning."

"We leave tomorrow morning," he repeated.

And then he kissed me.

And all those fantasies I'd had about kissing Jacob? About glasses removal and interlaced fingers and gentle embraces? Those slipped out of my mind as easily as a dream forgotten. The reality of this kiss was *so much better*. It felt impossibly good to have Jacob's arms around me and his lips—so soft, but so insistent—on mine.

Now that we were finally kissing, I couldn't imagine why our lips hadn't been locked all summer long.

I think Jacob felt that same regretful pang as we shifted from kiss to embrace. We sat there, our legs tangled in the sand and our arms wrapped tightly around each other. I laid my head on his chest and listened to his heartbeat.

"I guess I don't care that this is impossible," Jacob whispered into my hair. "Not anymore."

Then I was the one kissing him, with my fingers tangled in his hair and my body pressed against his and my mind filled with the sounds of the creek and the cicadas and Jacob's quickened breath. All those sounds swirled together like . . .

Like music.

And then it was a long time before I could think about anything at all.

But at some point, we drifted from kissing back to hugging and then, to talking.

"I forgot to tell you the other part of my plan," I told Jacob. "I want to come back to Camden next summer."

"Really?" he said.

I nodded.

"I want to teach," I said. "My own class, not assisting Nanny's. I mean, if they'll let me. I want to teach kids how to love music. How to make it their own, and nobody else's."

"But how can you do that without technique?" Jacob asked. "Isn't that kind of like running before walking?"

"Oh, there'll be technique," I promised. "They'll do so many scales, they're gonna feel like human escalators. But I'm also going to teach them to see music as a joy, not a chore."

I shrugged.

"It won't work for everybody," I said. "But for some kids, for the other me's out there, maybe it'll make a difference."

Jacob nodded slowly.

"It sounds amazing," he said. "Do you think Mrs. Teagle will let you do it?"

"Well, I *am* a Finlayson," I said, puffing out my chest and putting on a haughty voice.

"Yeah, you're also the girl she caught breaking into the infirmary," Jacob said.

"Oh, that," I said with a cringe. "Well, if Nanny *and* you vouch for my character? Do you think that'll help?"

"It better," Jacob said, drawing me close again. "Because I'm coming back too. I don't care how many groceries I have to bag, I'll be here."

I buried my face in his T-shirt, so happy. The only thing that stopped me from grinning was Jacob, kissing me again.

Even as we kissed, trying to make the moment last as long as possible, I could hear the burble of the creek. It danced in my head, along with the rhythm of our breaths, the low whistle of the breeze, and the beat of my happy heart.

TURN THE PAGE FOR MORE FLIRTY FUN.

My entire body ached as I stretched each limb and popped my back, trying to shake off the effects of the long, long trip. Cleveland to New York to London to here—I still couldn't believe we'd left home yesterday afternoon and had just arrived in Edinburgh's airport a couple of hours ago.

But as I stared out our hotel window overlooking Princes Street, with Scotland's rolling greens and ancient buildings staring back at me, the stiffness in my body faded away. I was really here. And it was breathtaking so far. I couldn't wait to see what other sights Scotland held.

There was a lovely park area in front of our hotel with rich green grasses and trees, and beyond the park there were rows of ancient-looking buildings lined along the street, pressed side by side with pubs, shops, and churches. This whole city was steeped in history. I was crazy excited to explore.

My mom stepped behind me and gave a soft sigh. "It's gorgeous, isn't it?"

I nodded my agreement. "Well worth being cramped in an airplane for this." I'd spent hours last week scouring online to find pictures, videos, anything to help get me ready for our two-week vacation to Scotland. But nothing could have prepared me for the image before me.

Downtown Edinburgh bustled with people below, and music and noise filtered up to us from the packed streets. I couldn't help but smile as I watched. Excitement swelled, and I was suddenly itching to get out there and walk. I wanted to touch the warm bricks with my fingers, smell the pub food and flowers, and hear the noises up close and personal.

"Ava," my dad said from behind me, "I printed you a copy of our itinerary. There's also a backup on your bedside table."

Mom chuckled, and we turned and faced my dad. He didn't show any signs of fatigue, since he'd slept like a log on our flight from New York to London last night. I, on the other hand, had gotten intermittent sleep, due to the snoring man on my right who apparently couldn't snooze unless his head was tilted my way.

Mom and I sat down on my bed, and we dutifully took our copies of the papers while Dad recited an overall rundown of how the trip would go. First we would spend a few days in Edinburgh and the surrounding cities, and Dad would spend some of that time doing research on our family heritage. Then we were taking a weeklong bus trip through Oban, Inverness, and St. Andrews so we could explore the Scottish Highlands.

The more he talked, the more excited he got, his eyes flashing bright.

"And if we stick to this schedule, we'll have plenty of time to fit in almost everything the experts agree we need to see," he concluded with a flourish. "We'll experience a good portion of what Scotland has to offer."

"This sounds like a pretty thorough sightseeing plan you've crafted. But do we get to sleep anytime in there?" Mom asked, her lips quirking with quiet amusement. "And maybe have a dinner or two as well?"

He rolled his eyes. "Don't be ridiculous. Of course we do. I scheduled an hour for each meal—it's listed clearly under each day."

An hour? Yeah, right. Mom was the slowest eater in the world. Apparently, he'd forgotten about this little fact. "Good luck policing Mom's eating speed," I told him with a hearty chuckle.

She shot me a mock glare, then grabbed her phone. Her fingers flew over the screen as she typed. "Laugh it up, smarty-pants. I just believe in savoring my meals. Anyway, I'm sending Mollie a text to let her know we've arrived. I'm so excited to see her. It's been far too many years since she and I have hung out."

During our travels here, Mom had given me some information about this family we were hanging out with in Scotland.

Apparently, Mom and Mollie had been best friends in high school. After they'd graduated and moved on to college, Mollie had spent a semester in Scotland her senior year. She'd fallen head over heels in love—both with the land and with a handsome guy she'd met on campus. The decision to stay here had been hard, but she hadn't looked back.

Mollie's family still lived in the Cleveland area, and Mom said she had coffee with her parents every once in a while. But Mollie herself hadn't been back to visit in years.

The way Mom talked about Mollie reminded me of my friendship with Corinne. Lasting and strong, no matter what happened in life. We'd known each other for years and had grown into best friends fast. Before I'd left for this vacation, she'd demanded I send her lots of pictures of my trip and keep her up to date on all the cute guys I saw. If only she could have come with me to experience Scotland too. She would love what I'd seen so far; the old buildings and rolling greens would appeal to her artistic nature. Talk about inspiration.

"So, Dad, where are you going to start your research?" I asked. He'd joined an ancestry website last year to begin building our family tree, and it was cool to see the old scanned birth certificates, pictures, and other artifacts regarding our ancestors.

"The National Archives of Scotland." He dug through his suitcase and produced a battered notebook. As he flipped through the pages, I saw his signature scrawl filling at least the first half of the notebook. Dad was nothing if not thorough and methodical.

"It'll get me a good start on which town we should narrow our focus down to. And someone online mentioned I can check out local churches as well, since they keep meticulous birth and death records."

After interviewing a number of family members and confirming the information online, Dad had traced our family line back to Scotland. When he'd casually brought up the idea of continuing his research in person, Mom and I had begged him for a family trip there until he'd caved. We'd all figuratively tightened our belts and cut back on spending to make sure we could afford it, with no complaints.

Yeah, I was willing to follow any goofy, overplanned agenda Dad set if it meant experiencing this. Even our hotel felt cool and different and older than anything I'd seen in America. This country breathed history, and I was full of anticipation to take pictures and draw it.

"Will we be able to find out our family tartan?" I asked him. It would be so cool to get a kilt made in it. Corinne would die of jealousy if I wore it to visit her—and probably tease me a little too.

He shrugged. "If we have one, I don't see why not. I don't think all Scottish families do, but maybe we'll be lucky."

My stomach growled, and I clapped my hands over it with a chagrined laugh. "Sorry."

Mom quirked her crooked smile and put her phone away. "Someone's hungry, it seems."

"Well, it has been a few hours since we ate lunch," I protested.

And even that had been a little lackluster—a plain sandwich and chips. I wanted a real dinner.

Dad scrunched up his mouth as he thought. "Well, we're not actually scheduled to start exploring Edinburgh until tomorrow, but I suppose we could get a taste of its foods right now and maybe do a little shopping—"

"Yes!" Mom and I said together, then laughed. We jumped off the bed and stood in front of Dad with pleading eyes.

He gave a heavy, resigned sigh. "Okay, fine. Put on your jackets, and let's go grab a meal. There's a place on High Street that was recommended by a number of people. We'll get some authentic Scottish cuisine there."

I slipped on my dark-blue fleece jacket and checked myself out in the mirror. My blond bob was a bit worse for wear but not horribly so, and a quick run-through of my brush smoothed the strays. I had on jeans and a T-shirt. Not my foxiest outfit ever, but it would do for now.

"You look lovely, Ava," Mom said as she walked by me, giving my upper arm a small squeeze.

We left the room and made our way down the hall, down the stairs, and into the large wood-trimmed lobby. A variety of people hustled and bustled around us, checking in as they dragged suitcases to the front desk, talking, laughing. Their energy was infectious, and I found my spirits lifted even higher.

Wow, I was in Scotland—I was really here! And this was going to be an awesome two weeks.

"Oh, just to remind you," Mom said to me when we stepped outside into the mild summer air. "Mollie and Steaphan have a son around your age. Graham. He'll be hanging out with us too," she added with a broad smile.

My good mood slipped a touch, and a hint of wariness filled me. Wonderful. Mom's attempts at vacation matchmaking weren't very subtle.

We crossed Princes Street and headed down the sidewalk toward High Street, weaving through the crowds of people. The air carried the rich scents of food and the sounds of drummers off in the distance. Sunlight peeked through intermittent clouds and warmed the air, which hovered around the midsixties. When we'd left Cleveland yesterday, it had been in the nineties and scorching hot for days. This was far, far more comfortable.

"I'm sure Graham is a nice guy," I finally said to Mom. My stomach growled again. I focused on my hunger in an attempt to change the subject. "So, I can't wait to try this restaurant. Do you think you'll try haggis while we're here? I don't know if I'm brave enough to eat it."

Mom ignored my food ramblings and continued, "You should give him a chance, Ava. I've seen Graham's pictures, and he's quite handsome. A clean-cut boy with a friendly smile."

"I'm sure he is." I knew the grin on my face was super fake, but I flashed it anyway. A mother's idea of handsome was quite different from a daughter's. Plus, I tended to like guys who were a little less prim and proper. David's short, scruffy black hair and dark-brown eyes came to mind, and I shoved the memory right back out again. At least that old sting in my heart didn't flare up at the thought of him, the way it had for so long after our breakup earlier this year.

Dad, who was already in tourist mode, had his camera at the ready and was busy snapping shots of the large brick and stone buildings lining the street. I took out my phone and snapped a few shots so I could send them to Corinne.

Mom nudged me with her shoulder and gave me a wistful smile. She was such a romantic. "I know what you're thinking, Ava, but who knows? Graham might turn out to be your Scottish vacation romance. After all, Mollie hadn't planned on falling in love, but here she is, almost twenty years later and still happy as a lark."

I gave her a casual shrug. Yeah, it would be awesome to find someone I liked that much, but I wouldn't hold my breath. I'd liked David too, a lot, and that had turned out terribly. No one else knew what had happened between us to make us break up, not even Corinne, and I wanted to keep it that way. The truth was far too mortifying. "We'll see," I replied with a broad smile. "I'm looking forward to meeting them all." That much was accurate, at least.